SEPARATE CASES

SEPARATE CASES

Robert J. Randisi

Walker and Company
New York

First published in the United States of America in 1990
by Walker Publishing Company, Inc.
Published simultaneously in Canada by Thomas Allen & Son
Canada, Limited, Markham, Ontario
Library of Congress Cataloging-in-Publication Data
Randisi, Robert J.
Separate Cases / Robert Randisi
ISBN 0-8027-5723-5
I. Title.
PS3568.A53S47   1990
813'.54—dc20   90-12018
CIP

Printed in the United States of America
2 4 6 8 10 9 7 5 3 1

This one is for Bill Pronzini
Because he's had a lot of things coming for a long time
and this is just one of them.

$\triangledown$

Prologue

" . . . And so it is your expert opinion, Mr. Jacoby, that Mr. Maxwell, as a licensed private investigator, could have acted in no other way?" Heck Delgado asked.

"Yes," I said. I mean that was my job, after all, to testify as an expert witness for Maxwell. That was the reason Heck had asked me to appear in court.

"Thank you for your cooperation, Mr. Jacoby." Heck turned to the District Attorney and said, "Your witness." That's when I got nervous.

I had never served as an expert witness before, not in my three years as a P.I., so it was only natural that I'd be nervous. At least, that was what Heck had told me. That and to try *not* to be nervous.

Fat chance.

The D.A.'s name was Richard Hilary—"Dirty Dicky" to his enemies—and he was not known for his easygoing manner. I'd checked his record when I found out he'd be cross-examining me. At fifty-one, Hilary was known as an ambitious ladder climber, and you didn't climb his kind of ladder by stepping *around* people—you did it by stepping *on* them. He was supposed to be very good at it.

He approached me, looking for all the world like he thought I was the next rung. Hell, he was even rubbing his palms together in anticipation.

"Mr. Jacoby, you are a licensed private investigator, is that correct?"

"Yes."

"Can you tell the court where your office is?"

I squirmed.

"Uh, I don't have an office."

"You don't have an office?" he repeated loudly.

"No."

"How do you meet clients, then?"

"Usually they call me and we arrange a meeting place."

"Call you where? At home?"

"Sometimes."

"If not at home, then where?"

"Uh, I sometimes get calls at a restaurant I frequent."

"What restaurant?"

"Bogie's."

"Bogie's?" he asked, frowning. "Isn't Bogie's a bar?"

"It has a bar, yes, but it's not—"

"I see," he said, smoothly cutting me off. "Mr. Jacoby, tell me, why do you not have an office?"

I squirmed again and looked at Heck. His face was expressionless. I tried to do the same with mine, but I could feel the perspiration on my forehead.

"I can't afford it."

"You can't afford it?" He repeated it loudly, as if the jury was hard of hearing.

"That's right."

"I see." He paced a bit, as if he had to think of another question, but I knew he had all of these questions set in his mind.

"Mr. Jacoby, were you ever a policeman?"

"No."

"Have you ever been a law enforcement agent of any kind?"

"No."

Dicky Hilary turned to the jury so they'd be able to see the puzzled look on his face.

"No?"

I chose not to repeat myself and just waited.

"Have you ever taken any kind of law enforcement course?"

"No."

"You have never attended, say, John Jay College of Criminal Justice?"

"No, I have not."

"Have you ever taken a home study course in law enforcement?"

"No."

Some of the jury members found that amusing and Dicky Hilary put a smile on his handsome face to show that he was one of them, and agreed with them.

"Mr. Jacoby, perhaps you will tell the court just what experience you have had in law enforcement?"

"I've had none."

"None," Hilary repeated, frowning. "I find that odd. Aren't many private investigators ex-policemen?"

"It's not a prerequisite for a license."

"Nevertheless, many of the men in your business have been policemen."

"I suppose."

"Would you tell the court—and the members of the jury—just what your profession was before you obtained your private investigator's license?"

This would go over like a lead balloon. I looked at Heck, but he was unable to do more than just look back. I was on my own.

"I was a fighter."

"A fighter? Er, what kind of fighter?"

"A prize fighter."

"Ah," Hilary said, as if he had just gotten it, "you were a professional boxer."

"I was."

"How many fights did you have?"

"Fifteen."

"Would you consider yourself a successful boxer, Mr. Jacoby."

"I won more fights than I lost."

Hilary chuckled and looked at the jury as he continued.

"So did the Mets last season, Mr. Jacoby, but that did not mean they had a successful season. In fact, most people considered them to be losers."

"I object," Heck said at that point. "Mr. Hilary is badgering the witness. I also object to this entire line of questioning. What Mr. Jacoby did before he became a private investigator is of no importance in this case."

"No?" Hilary asked. "Your Honor, I'm laying the foundation to challenge Mr. Jacoby's appearance here as a so-called 'expert witness.' I beg the court's indulgence for just a moment longer."

"Objection overruled," the judge said to Heck. He looked at Hilary and said, "You may proceed, Mr. Hilary."

"Thank you, Your Honor."

Yeah, thanks loads.

"Now, Mr. Jacoby, what was your won and lost record as a fighter?"

"I was twelve and three."

"That is, twelve wins and three losses?"

"That's correct."

"And how did you fare in your very last fight?"

"I lost."

"Well, how unfortunate. How did you lose?"

I pinned him with a hard glare that he ignored and said, "I was knocked out."

"Oh dear," Hilary said, showing the jury his best look of dismay. "And after having been knocked unconscious in that fight," Dicky Hilary continued, facing the jury, "you picked yourself up from the canvas and decided to become a private investigator." He turned dramatically to face me and said, "Isn't that correct?"

"It wasn't like—"

"No further questions, Your Honor."

"Redirect, Mr. Delgado?"

Well, sure, Heck stood up and allowed me to explain that I had worked for Eddie Waters for three years, acquiring the necessary experience for my P.I. ticket, and that getting knocked out in my last fight had absolutely nothing to do with my decision to change professions, but by that time the damage was done.

Ol' Dicky Hilary had moved himself up one more rung on the ladder.

$\triangledown$

1

I SIGHTED DOWN THE barrel at the silhouetted head of the figure in front of me and squeezed off three shots very deliberately. One shot took the figure between the eyes, and the other two went successively higher—one in the forehead and then a clean miss.

I put my next three shots in the figure's torso—heart, mid-chest, and belly, as aimed.

"You do a lot better when you're not trying to be fancy and hit the head, Mr. Jacoby," instructor Dan Turner said.

He was standing behind me and I turned to look at him as I ejected the six spent shells from my .38.

"Miles," I said for the hundredth time, "or Jack, or just plain Jacoby. Stop calling me Mr. Jacoby, Dan."

Turner was younger than me by only about five years, which, I guess, is why I objected to being called "Mister." If anything it should have worked the other way, since he was my instructor. A sharpshooter in the army, he was now one of the head instructors at the Chelsea Gun Club, located on Twenty-fifth Street and Eighth Avenue. For a twenty-five-year-old single guy, he was doing all right.

"Try putting six in the chest, Mis—Jack," he said. "That's what's going to stop the man for you. I've seen slugs—even thirty-eights and larger—just glance off a man's skull, which would leave him free to kill you."

"All right, Dan."

It had been three years now since the death of Eddie Waters—my mentor in the business, and much more—and the same period of time since I'd received my P.I. license. I'd had some interesting cases during that time. I'd learned quite a lot—and one of the things I'd learned was that once in a while you've got to carry a gun, and if you're going to carry a gun, you better damn well know how to use it. Point and shoot had been enough so far, but of late I'd decided to really learn how to use the damned thing—which I hated—and as a result of that I was in my second month as a member of the Chelsea Gun Club.

I sighted down the barrel and squeezed six times. You'd have needed a frisbee to cover the holes.

"Try to group them tighter, Jack," Dan said, and went on to his next student, a pudgy shopkeeper named Mr. Andros who was tired of being robbed.

Sure, I thought, ejecting the empties and reloading, easy for you to say.

I wasn't really a good student, which was part of the problem. My mind tended to wander while I was at the range, invariably to whatever case I was working on at the moment.

Normally, if I have one case I'm happy, because I'm eating. This was a rare time for me because I actually had two cases to work on, and they were stretching me beyond my limits.

Which was why I was at the range for an unscheduled session. I had to go someplace to think.

Earlier that day I was in Bogie's, a Manhattan restaurant on Twenty-sixth Street between Seventh and Eighth Avenues. It caters to a mystery crowd—that is, people who read, write, and publish mystery novels. They even have signed photos and book covers framed and hanging on the walls. Bogie's has become a home away from home for local and out-of-town writers. The owners, Billy and Karen Palmer, are friends of mine, and tolerate me hanging around there and using their phone.

I was sitting at the bar doing just that, waiting for a call from a street source named Binky. He was supposed to tell me where a hooker known as Two-John was holed up. Two-John was a hooker with a specialty; handling two johns at one time. Her real name was Jenny Wheeler. Heck Delgado—the attorney for whom I'd testified as an expert witness—had hired me to find her because he needed her to testify on behalf of one of his clients.

"Well, well," Stuart the bartender said as he set another bottle of St. Paulie Girl in front of me.

I looked at him and saw that he was looking at the front door. I looked that way and saw a woman coming in. She had long, graceful legs and dark brown hair that fell to her shoulders. She was fairly tall-five seven or eight. A very good-looking lady, but a little old to be from the Fashion Institute around the corner—unless she was an instructor. Maybe she was from CBS down the block.

"That's class," Stuart said.

"I thought you liked young bunnies," I said.

He frowned at me and said, "I am a class man all the way, Jack."

"I see," I said, sucking on the Paulie.

"Of course," he added, "if a young bunny with class happens to walk in . . ."

The class lady who was there now came walking down the bar and Stuart moved to meet her.

"Can I help you, Miss?" he asked. Suddenly, his Australian accent had gotten a bit thicker. I wondered if he used it on the ladies.

"My name is Caroline McWilliams," she said. "I'm looking for Miles Jacoby."

Stuart looked at me, not wanting to give me away if I didn't want to be given.

"I'm Jacoby."

Suddenly, she ignored Stuart—which not a lot of women do, because Stuart's a pretty good-looking guy. He's about my height, but several years younger, and a few pounds trimmer, with blonde hair and regular features. Stuart was not really a bartender at Bogie's; he was the manager filling in behind the bar.

Stuart usually made out pretty well with the ladies, but this particular lady only had eyes for me at the moment. I didn't let it go to my head.

"May I talk with you for a few minutes?" she asked.

"Sure."

"Privately?"

I looked at Stuart and said, "I'll be in my office," indicating the dining room and slid off the bar stool.

$\bigtriangledown$

2

Aᴄᴛᴇʀ ᴡᴇ sᴀᴛ ᴅᴏᴡɴ at a table, I asked, "Would you like a drink?"

"Is that any good?" she asked, indicating the Paulie Girl in my hand.

"If you like beer."

"I'll have one, please."

I made motions to Stuart to bring two Paulies to the table.

"What can I do to help you?"

She opened her purse and took out her wallet. From that she took a photostat much like the one I had in my wallet. I studied it and gave it back.

"So you're a lady P.I., huh?"

"There are such things, you know," she said, putting the photostat back in her wallet.

"Wait a minute," I said as bells started ringing in my head.

"McWilliams, McWilliams," I repeated. "Are you related to Andy McWilliams?"

She hesitated for a moment, then said, "I was his wife."

She used the past tense for a good reason. Andy McWilliams had been dead, if I remembered correctly, for about five months.

McWilliams had been a private investigator whose cases always made the papers—until somebody made the papers by killing him. The police attributed his murder to the Backshooter, a random, Son of Sam type killer who had been roaming the streets of New York's boroughs at night for about seven months.

"You've taken over the business?"

She nodded, and I refrained from mentioning that this gave us something in common, since I had taken over Eddie Waters's business after he was killed.

"I had to do something," she said. "I was going crazy. Andy made me apply for a license once as a joke. I never used it until after he was killed. I was like a zombie that first month, but four months ago I reactivated the agency. The first case I took was Andy's."

"To find out who killed him."

"Yes. I'm still working on it."

"You don't believe that it was the Backshooter?"

She shook her head.

"I think he was shot in the back to make it look like another Backshooter killing."

"I see. And what makes you think that?"

She stared at me a moment, then shrugged.

"Intuition, I guess."

"I see."

"Andy was jumpy the last few weeks before his death," she said. "Andy was never nervous about anything, Mr. Jacoby."

"Did he mention anything to you about what was making him jumpy?"

'No, he never discussed his business with me, unless it was necessary."

"I guess he didn't feel whatever it was he was jumpy about was necessary for you to know."

"Maybe he didn't want me to worry," she said, "but I did, nevertheless."

"Didn't you ever ask him about it?"

"No . . . I never asked Andy questions."

The ideal wife, I thought.

"I've worked on other cases as well, but whenever something comes up that I feel might lead me to Andy's killer, off I go again."

"Is that what brought you here? Another lead?"

"No," she said. "Frankly, Mr. Jacoby, I really don't think I can do it alone anymore. I'd like you to help me find Andy's killer."

"I see."

"You knew my husband."

"Not really."

"What's that mean?"

"Well, we worked on a case at the same time once. Not together, but at the same time. Needless to say, he solved it before I did. He was a brilliant investigator."

"Yes, he was," she said, but she said it without any enthusiasm. "What case was that?"

"It was just last year," I said, relating the details to her. It had been a kidnapping case where the father and mother were separated. McWilliams was hired by the father, and I was hired by the mother. The father had been better-off financially than the mother, which explained their choices pretty well.

"Andy was very impressed with you, but he didn't pronounce your name the way you do."

"Few people do," I said. The accent is on the "Jack", and not the "c-o." It's "Jack-uh-bee."

"He said that for someone as relatively inexperienced as you were, you showed good instincts."

Relatively inexperiences. Just then I was glad that she hadn't been in court last month when Dicky Hilary was tearing me apart.

"Thank you," I said. "That's very nice to know."

Before the conversation could progress any further, Stuart came over with the Paulies and a phone message.

"From Binky," he said, handing me a piece of paper on which he'd written the message.

"I didn't hear the phone ring."

He looked at Caroline, who was tasting the beer right from the bottle, and said, "I can see why."

"Thank, Stuart."

I looked at the piece of paper and saw that there was an address written on it for a hotel in Alphabet City.

"Mrs. McWilliams, I'm sorry, but I have to go."

"Wait!"

I got to my feet and said, "I don't really think I can help you. Your husband . . . Andy's been dead five months and it's a pretty cold trail. Besides, the police experts are sure it was the Backshooter."

"But it wasn't—"

"I'm sorry," I said. "I really have to go."

I headed for the bar and heard her chair scrape back as she rose to follow me.

"Stuart, can I borrow the phone?"

"Sure," he said, handing me the cordless.

I gave Heck a quick call and got his answering machine.

Obviously both he and his secretary, Missy, were out of the office. I left a message that I had a line of Two John's whereabouts and that I'd get back to him as soon as I knew something. I handed the phone back to Stuart, waved, and went out the door with Caroline McWilliams close behind.

"Mr. Jacoby—"

"Miles."

She had a long-legged stride that made it easy for her to keep up with me.

"Miles, I have to come with you."

"No way."

"We haven't finished talking."

"I'm afraid we have—"

"Listen!" she said sharply, grabbing my arm. "Andy mentioned you a couple of times. He really was impressed with you."

"With me," I repeated.

"Yes. He said you had more on the ball than most people."

I stared at her, wondering how high the bullshit was going to pile before she quit.

"Andy didn't like many people—"

"All, right, all right," I said, cutting her off. If I stood here all day arguing with her Two-John would get away—and I might drown. "Let's get a cab . . ."

$\bigtriangledown$

3

THE HOTEL WAS ON Fourteenth Street between Avenues
A and B. When we got there I put five bucks on the counter
for the clerk to salivate over and asked for Jenny Wheeler.

"Jenny who?"

"Wheeler," I said, adding a second five, "Two-John
Wheeler."

"Oh, Two-John," he said, taking the fives. "Room 304."

"Thanks."

"But she ain't there," he added as we headed for the stairs.

"What?"

"She cleared out last night."

"Did she say where she was going?"

"Nope."

"Let me have the key to the room."

"I can't—"

"For ten bucks you can—and don't tell me it was cleaned.

I might laugh in your face."

He shrugged and gave me the key. As we went up the stairs I caught a glimpse of him watching Caroline's legs. I didn't blame him, they were well-worth watching.

I opened the door to 304 and suddenly a lamp exploded against the wall next to my head.

Caroline screamed and I shouted, "Jesus!" and fell into a crouch. The guy who had thrown the lamp went out the window onto the fire escape.

"Take the stairs to the lobby!" I shouted at Caroline, then took off after him, hoping she'd react correctly.

When I hit the fire escape it was still quivering and seemed to be clinging precariously to the wall. I hoped if it fell I'd at least land on the guy I was chasing.

I heard him clamoring down the metal steps, and then I drowned him out with some clamoring of my own. Naturally he reached the alley below at least a floor ahead of me and took off in a dead run. He was in good shape and moving fast, so that's why it surprised me to see Caroline enter the alley ahead of him. I guess her long legs were good for more than just looking at. Unfortunately, once she came into the alley she didn't know exactly what to do. As the man reached her she put her hands out in front of her, anticipating the collision, but that didn't keep her from being knocked ass over tea kettle.

I hit the pavement and took off after him, but he was long gone by the time I got out of the alley. I went back to see how Caroline was.

I helped her up and she started apologizing right away.

"I'm sorry, but—"

"Forget it," I said. "As long as you're all right."

"I . . . I didn't know how to stop him," she said helplessly, trying to clean the dirt off her skirt.

"Next time drop to all fours and let him trip over you. Come on, let's check the room."

"But that man—"

"We interrupted him. Maybe there's something he didn't find."

We went back into the hotel by the front entrance. The clerk didn't give us a second look. I decided to let go the fact that he knew somebody was already up there when he let us up. After all, I'd waved money in front of him. How could he say no?

"Who was that man?" she asked as we went up the stairs.

"I don't know," I said. "I didn't get a good look at him. Did you?"

"No, I'm sorry—"

"Stop saying that!"

"I'm sorry . . ." I looked back at her and she said, "I'm sorry," again real quickly, and then clamped her hands over her mouth.

We entered the room and I gave it a quick once over. You couldn't tell anyone had ever been there. I was sure that the man ahead of us had found nothing either.

"She was here," Caroline said.

"How do you know?"

She showed me some red stained cotton balls she'd taken out of the waste basket in the bathroom.

"Blood?"

"No. She may be hiding out, but she still took the time to do her nails."

"Shit," I said. "I'm going to wring Binky's neck. Come on."

She dropped the cotton balls to the floor and we left.

Outside I said, "Well, I guess that's it, Caroline. Let's get a couple of cabs—"

"What do you mean?"

"Now we go our separate ways."

"Look, Miles, since Andy was impressed with your abilities you must be pretty good."

Yeah, I thought, an "expert." Just ask Dicky Hilary. "Thanks."

"I'm not just handing out compliments. Let's work together on this."

"On what, Caroline?"

"Andy's murder!"

"I work alone, Caroline. I told you, even though your husband and I once worked on the same case, we went our own ways." Wryly I added, "He always managed to be two steps ahead of me anyway."

"He said one."

"Fine, but I work my own way, and I work alone."

"It's because I'm a woman, right?"

It might have been, but I didn't want to admit that to her. Neither did I want to admit that my confidence was at an all-time low. Maybe I didn't want her around to see that. After all, she'd been married to Andy McWilliams.

"You've been in the business what, five months?" I asked.

"And what about you?" she shot back, lifting her chin defiantly. "A couple of years?"

Actually, I'd had my license for almost three years, but I didn't bother correcting her.

"I've had my license almost six years—" she began, but I cut her of before she could go any further.

"That's fine," I said, "but I'm sorry." I started walking away and she tagged along behind me like a kid, only she wasn't a kid. If I'm any judge of a woman's age, Caroline was in her mid-thirties, but she was hanging on my tail like she was twelve. And on top of everything else, she'd had her license longer than I'd had mine—which was just a technicality, but an annoying one.

"Miles, please, I need help! I can't do it alone!" Her tone had gone from plaintive to agonized. "I've been trying for five months and I'm not getting anywhere. Dammit," she said viciously, grabbing my arm and turning me around with surprising strength, "whatever happened to professional courtesy?"

She stopped following me then, but I only took a few more steps before turning and looking back at her. She looked harried and desperate. She had been in over her head for the past five months trying to make a murder out of something the police were calling a random killing and she was about to go under for the final time.

A cab came by then and I whistled it to a stop. She just stood and watched as I opened the back door.

"Get in," I told her.

"Oh, Miles," she said, gushing, "I can't tell you—"

"Just get in the cab, Caroline."

The first stop was Caroline's Madison Avenue office.

"What do you want from here?" she asked as she fitted the key into the door, which said MCWILLIAMS INVESTIGATIONS. She hadn't even had to change the sign when she reopened the office.

"Your file."

"Which one?"

"On Andy's case. You did keep a file, didn't you? You've been keeping it up to date, haven't you?"

"Oh, of course," she answered, a little too halfheartedly for my money.

She opened the door and we entered.

"This place looks like it's been searched."

She shut the door and her face took on a sheepish expression.

"It always looks like this."

"What?"

"I never claimed I was neat."

I was almost afraid to see what shape the files were in, but I forced myself to ask again for the one on Andy.

"It's in the cabinet—there."

I went to the cabinet she indicated and asked, "Which drawer?"

"The, uh, top one."

I opened the top drawer. It looked as if someone had emptied a waste basket in there.

"Caroline, all these scraps of paper—it looks like you're making confetti for a parade. How much of it has to do with Andy's case?"

"Um . . . all of it?"

"All of it?"

"I'm afraid so."

Christ.

"Okay, look," I told her, picking up the waste basket and dumping the contents on the floor, "take this and fill it with whatever papers you have on Andy's case. We'll sort it out at my place."

"Your place?" she asked, taking the waste basket from me. She looked funny standing there with it in her hands, her eyes wide and staring at me as if I'd just threatened her virtue.

"I meant my office." I didn't bother explaining that my office doubled as a restaurant—or vice versa.

I looked over her desk while she filled the can, but i knew I wouldn't find anything in that room. She had understated the fact when she said she wasn't neat.

"I should explain something to you," she said, setting the can down the desk.

"What?"

"I'm normally very competent," she said. "I can plan and execute dinner parties, I can balance my own checkbook, I can play softball, and I shoot a mean game of pool."

"Why are you telling me this?"

"Because I don't want you to judge me by the way this office looks," she said. "I'm the first to admit I'm out of my element here. I can't file or do office work, and my investigative abilities are small."

"Then why do this?"

"Because I have to find out who killed Andy," she said, "even if it means that I have to stumble around to do it. Can you understand that?"

I studied her for a moment and then said, "Sure, I can understand it, Caroline."

"Thanks."

"It's late," I said, picking up the can. "I'll take this home with me and look it over. You can go home and get some sleep and I'll call you in the morning."

"What will we do tomorrow?"

"I'm not sure yet. I want to talk to Heck Delgado, the attorney I'm working for, and I want to find the guy that sent me to Alphabet City, but beyond that I don't know yet. We can discuss that tomorrow."

Her apartment was on Eighty-second between York and First Avenues, and we rode all the way in silence. I was trying to figure out how to let her down easily, because working with her just didn't seem feasible. She may well have been competent in all other aspects of her life, but I only envisioned her getting in the way in this matter.

The cab stopped outside her apartment building. Before

she got out of the car she said, "I can't tell you how much I appreciate your help, Miles."

I smiled and said, "Just call it professional courtesy."

She got out, started to close the door, then stopped and poked her head back in.

"Here's my card with my home number," she said, handing it to me. "If you need help deciphering any of my notes, don't hesitate to call."

I stared after her as she entered the building, then looked at the number. I could barely decipher *that*.

4

AFTER DROPPING CAROLINE OFF, I stopped at the Chelsea Club, left the notes in my locker, and started my unscheduled practice.

I fired off six rounds and figured that was enough for one day.

"Finished?" Dan asked, coming up behind me.

"Yes," I said, ejecting the empties and reloading the gun. I shoved it in my shoulder holster, a rig I was still not comfortable with. Dan had suggested it in lieu of the belt holster I had used on the occasions when I did carry a gun.

"Harder to lose," he'd said, "sitting on a bus."

But uncomfortable as hell.

"You did real fine today, Jack. Been practicing somewhere else?" he asked.

"No," I said, "Just concentrating more, I guess."

Sure, I thought, concentrating on seeing D.A. Dicky

Hilary's face on every target. That made them real easy to hit. The paint job he'd done on me was a month old, but it was still churning my guts.

"See you next time then, Jack," he said, and went over to Mr. Andros, who had just missed his target with all six shots.

I reminded myself never to offer Mr. Andros a partnership.

Alison Hamer had helped me move into my new apartment, which was on Thirteenth Street and University Place, across the street from a deli and directly over a Pancake House.

Alison is twenty-six, and is cute *and* pretty, although she hates it when I call her cute. She has dark hair, pert (she hates that word, too) breasts, and the shapely-but-firm legs of a runner—which she is. She worked as a waitress at Bogie's, which was where we met, and we became friends— although not "close" friends. We were both a bit wary about that because I'd had my problems in the past, and I assumed she had as well, although she didn't talk about it much. We were friends, on our way to something else—but it was slow going.

Yes, we slept together on occasion, but a shared bed doesn't automatically make two people "close."

After my original apartment had been blown up in an attempt on my life—an attempt that killed my brother instead of me—I had moved into the back room of Bogie's, at Billy and Karen Palmer's invitation. When I finally found an apartment I had no sooner moved in when new owners bought the building and it went co-op. It had taken nearly five months to find another one I could afford. Because I'd had to give up Eddie Waters's old office—I couldn't afford that, either—I had also been using Bogie's back room as an office. Now that I had my apartment over the Pancake

House, I was out of the back room for good, easing my guilt about mooching off of the Palmers.

When I got back to my apartment Alison wasn't there, but the place was clean, so I knew she had been. I put Caroline's "files" aside for the moment, stowed the gun and rig in the closet, an dialed Alison's number.

"Hi," I said when she picked it up. "Thanks for cleaning up."

"It's all yours now," she said. "Everything is unpacked and in its place. Good luck."

"Thanks. When did you leave?"

"Actually, I just got home."

She lived within walking distance, on Horatio Street. It was a building I would have liked to see her get out of, but I guess I didn't want it badly enough to ask her to move in with me. I wasn't ready for that and, to be honest, I didn't think she was, either.

"I could come back," she offered.

"I'm really beat," I said.

"It's just as well. I start my new job tomorrow."

"That's right," I said, my memory jarred. No longer would she be waiting tables at Bogie's. She'd gotten a job at a TriBeCa art gallery that had its name printed on the window in lower case lettering, and she was very happy about it. She loved art and she knew it well. Since she couldn't paint, selling it was the next best thing.

"Talk about good luck," I said. "Break a leg."

"That only works in the theater, silly."

"Well, you know what I mean. Break an easel, or something."

"Thanks."

There was an awkward silence then. I finally broke it.

"Well, get a good night's sleep. You don't want to be late

on your first day."

"No, I don't."

"I'll see you, then."

"Jack?"

"Yeah."

"Are you . . . all right?"

Alison hadn't been in court with me last month, but she knew about it.

"Yeah, kid, I'm fine."

"Are you still . . . drinking?"

"Just a beer now and then, kid," I said. "Nothing serious."

I'd hung one on once or twice—or thrice—since the debacle in court. Not coincidentally, Alison and I had not seen as much of each other during that time.

"Sure," she said. "Nothing serious. I'll see you, Jack."

I hung up, wondering if we'd even be able to keep a friendship going, now that we'd be seeing so little of each other. Why had I been so inept at relationships over the years? The first woman I ever really fell in love with was my sister-in-law, for Chrissake. How was that for doing things right? Now my brother Benny was dead, and his wife Julie was gone.

Or was she?

God, I hadn't thought about Julie in ages. But instead of doing it now, I depressed myself even more by reading the *Post* while eating the roast beef sandwich I'd purchased from the deli across the street. I was waiting for the phone to ring, hoping Binky would give me a call again.

I opened the fridge, got out a can of Meister Brau, and popped the tab. It wouldn't be the last tab I popped that night. I meant to turn to the sports page and read Mike Lupica's column but ended up perusing the latest article on the Backshooter.

The Backshooter—as the newspapers had christened the killer who always shot his victims in the back—had first appeared seven months earlier. His first two victims, killed two months apart, had been connected immediately, not so much by the fact that they had been shot in the back—that *could* have been a coincidence—but by the fact that a playing card had been found on each body. Since then, a playing card had been found at the scene of two other murders in which the victim was shot in the back: The city had another Son of Sam on its hands.

The first two victims were killed out on Long Island, the third in Queens and the fourth, fifth and sixth—if Andy McWilliams was the fourth—in Manhattan. Now the seventh had been discovered only last night in Brooklyn. Seven victims in seven months.

Eddie Waters, from whom I learned almost everything I knew about being a detective, said that killers have massive egos. If that's the case, this one's ego was being fed by all the newspaper coverage, and that made me kind of sick.

I finished the sandwich and another couple of beers and went to bed. Caroline McWilliams "files" could be better faced after a good night's sleep.

I was comfortably ensconced in my bed before I realized that I had never gotten to Mike Lupica's column.

5

HECTOR DOMINGO GONZALES DELGADO'S office was at Madison Avenue and East Twenty-third Street. When I arrived he wasn't yet in, but I didn't mind passing the time with Missy, his beautiful, red-haired, thirty-year-old secretary.

Missy used to be Eddie Waters's secretary and lover. After Eddie was killed and I found his killer, Missy took work with a temporary outfit, the kind that sends people on a different job every day. I couldn't afford to keep her as my secretary, but I did keep her as my friend. She eventually got a job with Heck and the two hit it off immediately.

Heck is a handsome young lawyer with a Ricardo Montalban accent. I wouldn't have faulted them for forming a relationship other than employer and employee, but I couldn't honestly say I knew that they had.

We talked for about fifteen minutes before Heck finally arrived. Missy asked me how I was doing more than once.

Being Heck's secretary, she knew all about my first appearance as an "expert witness."

I told her I was fine each time she asked, but she didn't believe me. Finally, Heck arrived.

"Good, you're here," Heck said. "That means you've found something."

"We have to talk."

Heck frowned.

"I guess that means you haven't found out anything."

"It might all be in the telling."

"Good morning, Missy," he said, looking past me. "Would you get out the Scalesi brief, please?"

"And coffee?"

"Yes, please."

"Right away."

She didn't offer me a cup because I already had one in my hand. She'd given me a cup that said NUMBER 1 SECRETARY on it. She was using the one that said 1986 METS, WORLD CHAMPS. It occurred to me then that I'd known both of these people for a number of years, and didn't know which one of them was the Mets fan.

"Come inside," Heck said, and entered his office.

I went in behind him and watched as he hung up his coat, then opened his attache case—real leather-and took out some papers and folders.

When Heck hired me to find Two-John we had not discussed his client's case. It was enough for me to know that he wanted to find her, and that he'd pay me to do so.

That had changed.

"What happened?" he asked.

"Did you get my message?"

"What message?"

"The one I left on your machine."

"No," he said, and buzzed Missy. When she came in he asked if she had gotten a message from me on the answering machine.

"Only this morning," she said. "I left a note on your desk." She pointed to it, and he picked it up and scanned it.

"So you did. All right, thank you, Missy." After she left he said to me, "Neither of us was in the office much yesterday, Jack. Tell me what happened."

"Has your client ever had anything to do with a P.I. named Andy McWilliams?"

"McWilliams?" he said, frowning. "Wasn't he one of the Backshooter's victims?"

"So they say."

"What do you mean?"

"His wife doesn't seem to think he was. She's a licensed P.I. and she's asked me for help in finding his real killer."

"What has that got to do with my client?"

I told him about meeting Caroline McWilliams, and how she said she'd gotten a tip that Two-John knew something about her husband's death. I didn't bother mentioning the guy who was in training for the Olympic lamp throwing competition.

"You didn't find her, so you couldn't ask her," Heck said.

"That's right, but I'm asking you. What dealings did your client have with McWilliams?"

Tapping his pen on his desk Heck said, "I'd have to ask him."

Missy entered at that point, putting a cup of coffee and a folder on Heck's desk. Heck's cup said I LOVE MY BOSS, with a red heart where the word LOVE should be.

"What's your client's name, Heck?"

Heck sipped his coffee and studied me carefully over the cup's rim.

"Scalesi," he said finally. "Salvatore Scalesi."

"The Mafia Scalesi?" I asked. "The one who's on trial for doing in his wife?"

I remembered reading about the case, and that Heck was the attorney, but I hadn't thought I was working on that case when I accepted the job of locating Two-John.

"Does that make a difference?" he asked.

"Not to me," I said. "But it *is* interesting."

"Jenny Wheeler can prove that my client didn't kill his wife," Heck said.

"That's what Scalesi says."

"Yes."

I put my cup down on his desk and shrugged.

"I'll keep looking."

"I'll ask him about McWilliams."

"I'd appreciate it."

I stood up and prepared to leave.

"Are you helping her?" Heck asked. "Is that what this is about?"

"Partially."

"The cops have chalked McWilliams up as another one of the Backshooter's victims, haven't they?"

"They have," I said, "but she's pretty certain he wasn't. She's been working for months on that assumption. Somebody gave her Jenny Wheeler's name as a source for information about her husband's death. That same somebody called her and sent her to Bogie's to find me. I'd really like to find out who that somebody is."

"It would be interesting," he admitted. "Keep me informed, will you?"

"Sure."

I started for the door, then turned and said, "Heck?"

"Yes?"

"You know, if you wanted to put Walker Blue or someone else on this, I'd understand."

"Jack," Heck said, pinning me with a hard stare, "how many times do I have to tell you, forget what happened in court last month."

"That's easier said than done, Heck," I said. "I cost you a case—"

"That case was a lost cause from the start," he said. "Bringing you in as an expert witness was just a longshot."

"You didn't know just how much of a longshot it was, did you?"

"I don't want to hear any more of this," he said, dismissing my self-pity. "Get out there and find me Two-John Wheeler."

"Okay," I said. "I'm gone."

"Where are you off to now?"

"The Seventeenth Precinct."

"Hocus?"

I nodded. "I'd like to see what he knows about the Backshooter case, or what he can find out," I said.

"I'll call you after I've talked to my client."

"I appreciate it, Heck."

He nodded, and opened a folder on his desk. I went into the outer office and said good-bye to Missy.

The Seventeenth Precinct is on East Fifty-first Street, between Third and Lexington. It is also called Midtown South, and is the headquarters for the Major Case Squad, to which Detective Hocus and his partner Wright were now assigned. It was also the headquarters for the special task force that had been formed to try to find the Backshooter. Hocus wasn't part of that unit, nor was his partner. Still, they might have some information for me. If I asked nicely.

$\triangledown$

6

As USUAL I WALKED into the Precinct with a bag of hot coffee containers. The cop on the desk was someone I was familiar with—and to—so I left one with him. I took the rest up to the Major Case Squad Room with me.

Hocus was at his desk, his shirt sleeves rolled up. He looked harried, which was not surprising, considering the amount of work there is in New York City for someone assigned to Major Case. There were a couple of other cops siting at desks in the room, but none of them paid me any mind.

"Where's your better half?" I asked.

He looked up at me with red-rimmed eyes and said, "If you don't have coffee in that bag you'd better head right back out that door."

I took out a container and handed it to him, saying, "Surprise."

He reached for it. "Got more in there?"

"For your partner."

"He doesn't drink coffee anymore. Besides, he's not here. Gimme."

I gave him the second container.

"What else is in there?"

"Mine—and don't say gimme, 'cause you can't have it."

"Have a seat," Hocus said. "I could use a break."

I sat.

"I heard Dicky took a bite out of you."

"Word gets around," I said, sourly.

"Don't let it bother you," he said. "We all carry his scars."

"Thanks," I said, not bothering to tell him that it didn't help to hear that. "What are you working on these days?"

"Name it. Arson, homicide, drugs."

"Poor baby."

"That's what my wife says," he said. "It sounds a lot nicer when she says it."

"I'll bet you're usually in bed when she does."

"Coffee doesn't buy you the story of my private life," he said. "Just what is it that you *do* want this coffee to buy for you, Jack?"

I shrugged.

"I was just wondering what you knew about the Backshooter case."

"Nothing," he said, "and I don't want to know anything. I've got enough problems without working on a killer case like that. A *random* killer," he said, shaking his head. "Jesus, that's the worse case of all to have. Who knows where he's going to strike next?"

"Only he does, I guess."

"Yeah, maybe." He sipped his coffee morosely, then looked at me and said, "That it?"

"Did you know a P.I. named McWilliams?"

"McWilliams? Andy McWilliams?"

"That's him."

"I knew of him," Hocus said. "I never crossed paths with him. Weren't he and Walker Blue supposed to be the best in the business?"

"They were."

"From his rep, he and Blue were two very different people," Hocus said.

"What do you mean?"

"Blue's sort of a stiff-necked type, isn't he?"

"Yes."

"Well, McWilliams sure as hell wasn't."

Now that Hocus had mentioned that, I remembered attending a convention in Canada where McWilliams had a blonde on his arm. He had to have been married at that time, which meant he certainly was not stiff-necked.

"He was shot, wasn't he?" Hocus asked, and then he raised his eyebrows and said, "Wait a minute. He was one of the Backshooter's victims."

"That's what they say."

Hocus frowned and said, "What do you mean, 'they say'?"

"Well, his wife doesn't think he was just another random victim of the Backshooter."

"What does she think?"

"I guess she figures that somebody who knew what he was doing killed her husband."

"Maybe it was a jealous husband."

"Then you don't think he was a Backshooter victim?"

"Whoa," Hocus said, holding up both hands, "I was just kidding around. I told you I don't know anything about the Backshooter case."

"Well, who does?"

Hocus smiled then, and I didn't like the way it looked.

"What?" I said.

"A good buddy of yours is on the Backshooter Task Force."

"Who?"

"Vadala."

"Oh, Jesus."

Detective Pat Vadala hated P.I.s in general, and me in particular. He was somebody I went out of my way to avoid.

"Anybody else I can talk to?"

"Let me think—yeah, as a matter of fact. You know Steve Stilwell?"

"I don't think . . . wait—"

"Sure, you know Steve," Hocus said, prompting me. "He's about your height, thin as a rail, tries real hard to grow a beard. Looks sort of scraggly."

"He worked Narcotics, didn't he?"

"That's right. I guess that scraggly look came in handy then."

"He's on the task force?"

Hocus nodded. "Working the streets."

"Can you put me in touch with him?" I asked. "Set up a meeting?"

"If he's willing, sure."

"Let me know, will you?" I said, standing up.

"Okay, Jack," Hocus said. "Uh, before you go, you want to take a little advice?"

"Sure, Hocus, I'll listen."

"Wives—widows—don't usually think rationally about their husband's deaths—especially when it was a violent death. Don't put too much time in on this. You're liable to be disappointed."

"I'll keep it in mind. Thanks."

Hocus nodded. "I'll call you when I've talked to Stilwell."

He dove back into the pile of cases he had on his desk, and I left.

$$\triangledown$$

7

I WAS IN MY apartment looking over the paper I'd gotten from Caroline McWilliams's office files when the phone rang.

"Jacoby."

"Jack, it's Hocus."

"Gee, I haven't spoken to you for hours."

"Still want to talk to Stilwell?"

"Oh, yeah."

"Seven P.M.," Hocus said.

"Tonight?"

"Yup."

I checked my watch and saw that it was five-thirty already.

"Where?"

"Uptown, west side. A restaurant called 'The Brothers'. Know it?"

"No, but I'll find it."

"Broadway, the corner of Eighty-seventh."

"Thanks, Hocus."

"It's gonna cost you a dinner."

"Cheap at the price."

"You think," Hocus said. "Stilwell may be skinny, but he eats like a horse."

"I'll chance it. Thanks again."

I hung up and rubbed my eyes. I'd been going over Caroline's papers since returning from Hocus's office. All I had to show for it was a headache.

I had to give her credit, though. Even though the papers were in a state of disarray and her handwriting was terrible, she *had* documented everything she'd done over the past five months to look into her husband's death. Unfortunately, I couldn't see any connection with Two-John Wheeler. The next thing I was going to have to do was ask her for the files that had been active when her husband died.

I got up from my desk and went to the refrigerator for another beer. I staggered a bit, but wasn't smart enough to figure out what that meant—not right at that moment. I drank the beer, thinking about Dicky Hilary, then put on my jacket and went out.

When I got to the restaurant Stilwell was already there. He looked slightly more presentable than a bum off the street. He'd hung up his soiled, green army jacket and was sitting there in a red plaid lumberjack shirt, which hung on him like it was his older—and bigger—brother's. He still had that straggly beard, too.

A maitre d' came to seat me, but I told him I was meeting someone.

"Is that your friend, sir?" the man asked, looking at Stilwell.

"I'm afraid so."

The man gave me a dubious look, then motioned me to the table.

The restaurant was split in two. The half we were in was for dinner, and the other half was more of a diner set-up, used mostly for breakfast and lunch. The area around the restaurant was under heavy construction, and business was good. Maybe Stilwell could have passed for a construction worker, but he still looked like a bum.

"Stilwell," I said, sitting opposite him.

"Sorry if I'm destroying your reputation,' he said, looking up from a menu.

"It can't get much worse than it is. Are you ready to order?"

"You haven't seen a menu yet," he said, offering me his.

I waived it away and said, "I'll have what you have."

"You might regret that."

"I'll chance it."

I waved for a waiter and one came quickly. I guess they figured the faster they served us the faster they'd be rid of us.

Stilwell ordered a roast beef sandwich, french fries in brown gravy, French-cut string beans, a salad with creamy garlic dressing, coffee, and a glass of Diet Coke.

"Diet Coke?" I asked.

He just shrugged.

"And you, sir?" the waiter said.

"The same, but I'll have a beer."

"We have Bud, Bud Lite, Miller, Miller Lite, St. Paulie Girl—"

"I'll have a Paulie Light," I said. Paulie didn't make a "lite" beer, but they did have "dark" and "light." He nodded, took Stilwell's menu, and left to put in our order.

"Hocus said you needed some information on the Back-shooter case," Stilwell said. He had gentle brown eyes that looked out from behind wire rim glasses. He made a good undercover because no one would ever guess that this slender, bookish-looking man in his thirties could be a cop.

"I appreciate you meeting me."

"No sweat," he said. "A free meal is a free meal."

I thought maybe he'd been working the streets too long, but I didn't say anything.

"What do you need?"

"I'm interested in one specific shooting."

"Which one?"

"McWilliams."

"The P.I."

"Yeah."

He frowned and asked, "Why? You're not thinking of looking for this guy are you?"

"No way," I said. "I'll leave that to the police. No, McWilliams' wife came to me. She doesn't think he was a random victim."

"She thinks somebody else killed him and tried to make him look like a Backshooter victim?"

"Either that, or the cops are just wrong."

He shrugged and said, "It's not like that's never happened. So you're working it from the other end?"

"I'm just trying to get her some information," I said. "I'm not putting a lot of time into this."

"Well, I don't know what I can tell you. The M.O. on the McWilliams shooting fit our man to a tee," he said. "We didn't have any reason to believe otherwise."

"Same caliber gun used?"

He hesitated, then said, "No."

"Well then—"

At that moment the waiter came in with some pickles, breadsticks, and other condiments.

"This hasn't been in the papers, Jacoby," Stilwell said, after the waiter left, "and it shouldn't go past this table."

"You've got my word."

"The guy uses a different caliber gun each time."

"No repeat?"

"He repeats, but never the same two in a row. The first victim was killed with a .44 Mag, the next one with a .38. After that he used a .32, the forty-four again, and a nine millimeter. I may not have the right order, though."

"Anything else?"

"He's stuck with those four, so far, but that doesn't mean he won't introduce another one on us—next time."

"What was McWilliams shot with?"

He frowned and said, "I'd have to check on that and call you."

"I'll give you my number."

"I'll get it from Hocus."

We talked a little bit more about the case—about what a headache it was, and about how he hoped they'd luck onto something the way the cops did with Berkowitz.

"Or maybe the fucker will just stop," he said, but he didn't sound too hopeful of that.

The waiter came with our dinners and I watched as Stilwell packed it away. When he realized I wasn't going to finish my string beans he asked if he could have them. He also finished my salad. I had another beer with dinner, and another after. By the time we were finished, my head was buzzing.

"What else you working on?" he asked.

"You know, you might be able to help me with this too," I said.

"What?"

"I'm looking for a working girl named Two-John Wheeler."

He nodded and said, "I know her. What do you need her for? This case?"

"No, I've been hired by an attorney who needs her for a witness."

"Good luck," he said. "Two-John's never been to court as a witness, just a defendant."

"If you happen to get a line on her, would you let me know?"

"Does she know you?"

"Yeah."

"If I see her, I'll tell her to call you, and I'll let you know where I saw her."

"Okay, fine," I said. Hell, I didn't expect him to sit on her. He was a cop, and cops usually need some kind of probable cause to do that.

"We're getting the eye," I said, looking over at the maitre d'.

"Fuck him," Stilwell said. "The food wasn't that good, anyway." I agreed, but I wondered how much he would have eaten if it had been good.

As we stood up it was me who made like a bum, and not him. I staggered, grabbed for a chair, and knocked it over. We got some attention from the other diners.

"You all right?" he asked.

"Fine."

"You're not driving are you?"

"I'll take the subway."

He took my arm as a waiter came over to pick up the chair I'd knocked down.

"I'll put you in a cab."

"You don't have to—"

"Come on."

I paid the bill, painstakingly counting out the money, including a small tip, and then he steered me outside. I had gotten colder and the breeze felt good and cleared my head a bit.

"Three beers always do that to vou?" he asked.

"Those three, three I had at home—it adds up."

He whistled up a cab and then guided me to the back door.

"I'll call you with the info," he said as I got in.

"Appreciate it," I said. He slammed the door for me and suddenly, in the warm interior of the car, I was very tired.

"Where to, pal?" the cabbie asked.

"Uh, Thirteenth and University Place."

"Gotcha."

He had to wake me up when we got there.

8

I WOKE EARLY THE next morning with a craving for cold orange juice. I had three large glasses, which did almost nothing to satisfy my craving. I thought about breakfast, but my stomach rebelled at the thought. I went back to bed instead.

When I woke again it was almost eleven. I took a shower, then went out to get breakfast. It was very cold outside, and the chilled air did me good. I walked across the street to the deli and ordered a container of black coffee.

There were two women behind the counter as usual, one middle-aged, the other young and pretty. Both were dark-skinned and dark-haired, and could have been mother and daughter. I'd always meant to talk to the young one and ask her what her name was, but I never had. She smiled at me like she always did and handed me my coffee, telling me to have a nice day.

One of these days I *would* ask her name.

I drank the coffee while walking to Bogie's and was finished by the time I got there. They weren't really open yet, not for a few more minutes, but Stuart saw me and let me in. I sat at the bar and asked the waitress, Vivian, for a black coffee. Vivian was a switch from the sweet, young things they usually hired at Bogie's. She was older than the other waitresses and more reliable. She was also a very handsome woman.

"You look like shit," Stuart said.

"Nice to see you, too," I said, as Vivian put the coffee down next to my elbow with a smile.

I reached into my pocket for Caroline's phone number. I tried to read it, but my eyes weren't focusing properly.

"Do me a favor," I said to Stuart, handing him the card. "Hand me the phone and read that to me."

Stuart handed me the cordless phone they had taken to keeping behind the bar and read the number off to me.

"Wonderful handwriting," he said, passing it back.

I tucked it away and said, "Don't pull my leg. She writes like a chicken."

"I didn't know chickens could write."

"I rest my case."

"Hello?" Caroline said.

"Caroline, it's Miles."

"Hello, Miles. Have you . . . found out anything?"

"I'm afraid not. Listen, I'd like you to do something for me."

"What?"

"Get together whatever active cases Andy was working on when he died. I'll pick them up later."

"When?"

"I don't know— Can we meet at your office at, say, six?"

"Sure. I'll have everything ready by them."

"Fine. I'll see you then."

I disconnected before she could reply.

"The long legs from yesterday?" Stuart asked, taking the phone back.

"Yes."

"You don't seem very anxious to see her."

"I'm not all that anxious to see anyone these days."

"I've noticed that you're in something of a blue funk these days."

"It'll pass, I guess." At least, I hoped it would.

Maybe if I went to see Dicky Hilary . . . No, that wouldn't do any good. Maybe he was right about me. Maybe I should get back into boxing, as a cornerman, or maybe as a trainer or manager.

"Where are you going?" Stuart asked as I climbed down off the stool.

"To see an old friend," I said.

One who probably never expected to see me again.

"I never expected to see you again," Willy Wells said. "Not here, anyway."

Wells, who was in his late sixties, was a grizzled veteran of what some people like to call "the ring wars." A light-weight in his younger days, Willy fought Willie Pep for the title once, and still swears that he was robbed by a bad decision. After that he became a cornerman, and eventually a trainer. He was acknowledged as the best in the business, having trained five world champions, including a kid who came out of the 1980 Montreal Olympics to eventually win titles in three different weight classes.

"How are you, Willy?"

The smell of Forty-second Street Gym brought back memories. The last time I had been there was to try my hand at sparring, only I'd been grossly out of weight. Following a dressing down by Willy for letting myself go—and offer a case that brought me in contact with karate—I had gotten myself back into shape, but never returned to sparring. I was now somewhere between the two conditions—not *in* shape, but not as badly out of shape as I once was.

"What kind of shape are you in?" he asked. "You look like you've dropped some weight since the last time I saw you." He was watching one of his fighters work a few rounds in the ring, but with just a glance he'd noticed that I was significantly slimmer than the last time I'd seen him.

"Some," I said, "and put some back."

"How far off your fighting weight are you?"

"About ten pounds." And I'd put every ounce of it on since the debacle in court.

"Shouldn't be too hard to take off. Are you looking to spar a little, or make a comeback?"

"A comeback?" I said. "Give me a break."

He shrugged and said, "Figured maybe you'd seen all the money they're throwing around these days. White fighter could make himself a pretty penny—if he was in shape."

"I have been thinking about getting back into the game, Willy, but not as a fighter."

"What then?"

"Cornerman, maybe."

"Cornermen are a dime a dozen," he said, treating my remark to a flip of his hand. "There's no money in it."

He wasn't being quite truthful. A good cornerman is worth his weight in gold, but maybe he was saying I wouldn't make a good one.

"Take my advice," he said, still watching his fighter carefully. "Take off the weight and think about a comeback. You're still young enough to make some serious money. Look at Big George Foreman."

Foreman, the old heavyweight champ, was twenty fights into a comeback at age forty, and had won all but one by knockout. I wasn't yet thirty-two. I probably should have been encouraged by that fact.

But I wasn't.

Now that I was here, my reason for coming seemed silly, and the idea of a comeback seemed even more ridiculous.

"What are you trying to tell me, Willy?"

He turned and faced me.

"I ain't tryin' to tell you nothin', kid. I'm just thinking out loud."

"If I wanted to come back, would you be willing to train me? Is that what you're saying?"

"If you wanted to come back," he said, "I'd be willing to take a look at you—but you have to take off the extra weight first," he added, poking me in the stomach.

"Willy, at my age—"

"What are you, an old man?" he asked, caustically. He turned back to watch his fighter in the ring. He was a young Hispanic welterweight with quick hands.

"I'll let you know what I decide, Willy."

He looked at me quickly, then back at his fighter.

"Don't wait too long," Willy said. "The old skills rust if you don't use them."

"I'll keep that in mind."

9

I SHOWED UP AT Caroline's office at six-fifteen and found the door locked.

"Sorry I'm late," I said as she let me in.

"Forget it."

"You won't do much business if you keep the door locked."

"I'm not worried about that," she said. "I have those files for you."

She walked to her desk. On top of it was a cardboard box, and inside were the files. These, having been maintained by Andy and not her, were in much better shape. Neatly typed, meticulously maintained.

"You can take them with you and keep them as long as you like."

"What about your own cases?"

"What about them?"

"Any connection with Andy?"

"No, I took on those cases myself, after he . . . he died. Oh, some of them were old customers—they weren't so sure about hiring me, but I managed to convince them."

"And do the job."

"For the most part."

"How many cases are you working on right now?"

"I don't have any at the moment."

And she wouldn't, not as long as she kept her door locked.

"You should keep busy, Caroline."

"I know," she said, but didn't offer any word on whether she intended to or not.

"Have you . . . talked to anybody?" she asked.

"I spoke to a couple of police contacts about the Back-shooter case. I'm expecting some information soon."

"Will you call me as soon as you know something?"

"Sure."

She sat down behind the desk, looking like she intended to be there a while.

"Look, Caroline, before I take these back to my place I'm gonna get something to eat. Would you like to come along?"

"I'm really not very hungry, Miles," she said, smiling wanly. "Maybe another time."

"Okay, another time," I said, picking up the box.

"Here, let me get the door," she said, rising from behind the desk.

I passed through the doorway and said, "Thanks."

"Thank you, Miles. I mean it. I really appreciate—"

"I'll call you, Caroline."

She was gushing again, and that made me uncomfortable. I mean, I still wasn't so sure I was going to do her all that much good, and then all that gushing would go to waste.

I meant to go right home with the files and go through them, but when I got into the cab I gave the driver the address of Bogie's.

Two hours later Stuart came over to where I was seated at the bar and said, "Come on, Jack. Go home."

"After another beer."

Stuart looked over at Billy Palmer, who was standing at the far end of the bar, and then said to me, "No more, Jack. I'm cutting you of."

I looked at him and asked, "Are you cutting me off, or is Billy?"

"Does it matter?" he asked. "You can't get another drink here tonight."

"Then I'll go someplace else," I said. But who was I kidding? I made no move to get off the bar stool.

I felt a hand on my shoulder and turned to find Billy standing next to me. His brown eyes looked tired and his bushy moustache was drooping more than usual.

"How about letting me get you a cab?" he asked. "Or better yet, why don't you have something to eat."

"How's business?" I asked.

"Rotten."

"All right," I said, "I'll have something to eat. Fettucini Alfredo, with the chicken and broccoli."

"Charlie's speciality," Billy said, slapping me on the shoulder. "Coming up."

After Billy left Stuart came over and leaned on the bar in front of me.

"No hard feelings?"

I looked at him and said, "Don't worry, I'm not a nasty drunk—yet! Gimme a Diet Coke."

1 0

WHEN I WOKE UP the next morning I was glad Stuart and Billy had cut me off. If they hadn't, I'd have had a worse headache than I did.

I brewed myself a pot of coffee and made some calls, trying to locate Binky. It wasn't inconceivable that he was hiding out from me. Finding a missing person was bad enough, but the last thing I needed was to try to find someone who didn't want to be found. That was virtually impossible.

Over coffee and English muffins—the only thing my stomach didn't lurch at the thought of—I went over Andy McWilliams's open files. There were six—Jesus, I thought, six cases at one time?—but that wasn't exactly right. As it turned out he had subcontracted three of the cases.

One he had given to Henry Po, a friend of mine who usually investigated cases involving thoroughbred horse racing, but who did take some work on the side. He had taken some in the past from me. This one had to do with a man who worked for a stock brokerage firm near the World Trade Center who might have been ripping-off clients.

The second case was for a client in New Jersey. McWilliams had given it to a P.I. named Malone, who I didn't know. This case involved the possibility that a betting clerk at the Meadowlands was passing out winning tickets—after the race was over.

The third case he gave to another P.I. I knew, and it came as quite a surprise to me. I didn't know this particular man took on work from other P.I.s. It was Walker Blue.

Since McWilliams and Blue were considered two of the best in the business, that might have had something to do with Blue taking the case, but it sure couldn't have been out of friendship. The lifestyles of the two men were as different as night and day—and besides, I didn't think Walker Blue had any friends. He just wasn't the type.

None of those three cases had been closed out after McWilliams's death. I'd have to ask Caroline if she knew what had happened with them. Failing that I'd have to ask the individual investigators, Po, Malone, and—as previously indicated—Walker Blue.

The three cases that McWilliams had been working on himself and all been referred to other investigators by Caroline, two to Walker Blue, and one to a man I knew in Brooklyn, Nick Delvecchio. The final disposition of those cases was not indicated. Again, I'd probably have to talk to the individual investigators.

I picked up the phone and dialed Caroline's number. It was the only one she'd given me, and I hoped it was her home number. That would be the only place I'd find her this early.

The phone rang six times, and I was about to hang up when she answered.

"Um, hello," she said, breathlessly, sleepily. For a moment I wondered if I had interrupted something, but then I put that thought aside. It had only been five months since Andy's death, and Caroline hadn't struck me as a woman who had put her husband's death behind her.

"Caroline, it's Miles," I said. "Are you awake?"

"I will be . . . in a minute," she said.

I gave her the minute and she sounded more alert when she came back on.

"What's wrong?"

"Nothing's wrong," I said. "What can you tell me about these active cases of Andy's?"

"Which ones?"

"Didn't you read them over when you took them out for me?"

"No," she said, admitting it a bit sheepishly, "I just pulled the cases he was working on when he was . . . when he died."

I closed my eyes, then opened them and looked at the files that were spread out across my kitchen table.

"Caroline, how well did Andy know Walker Blue?"

"They worked together sometimes. They also referred cases to each other. Wait a minute. I referred two of those cases to Walker, didn't I?"

"Yes, and Andy had him working on one before he died. Do you know the disposition of any of these cases?"

"Could you, you know, read them to me?"

I gave her the gist of the two cases she had referred to Walker, but I told her I didn't know what the first one was, the one Andy himself had asked Walker to look into.

"I don't know what Walker did on those cases, and I'm afraid I don't know about the one Andy gave him. He didn't talk about his work."

She wasn't much help, but I refrained from telling her that.

"I suppose you don't know about the case you referred to Nick Delvecchio, either."

"I don't know Delvecchio," she said. "I only know that Andy liked him, so I sent him a client."

For a moment I wondered if McWilliams had ever considered farming a case out to me—and why he hadn't. I decided not to ponder that. My self-confidence was low enough.

"I'm sorry, Miles," she said. "I really don't know what happened with any of those cases."

"You didn't work on any of them yourself?" I asked hopefully.

"No," she said. "After Andy died I just referred his open cases and closed the office. I didn't decide until a week later to run the office myself."

Yeah, I thought, into the ground.

"All right," I said. "I'll have to talk to these other P.I.s myself."

"Do you know them?"

"All but the guy in New Jersey. I'll have to call him. Hold on a minute." I checked the file, but the New Jersey P.I.'s phone number wasn't there. "When you're in the office, check Andy's rolodex and get me the number for Malone in New Jersey. Okay?"

"What's the first name?"

"It just says, 'subbed to Malone,'" I said. "There can't be more than one."

"I'll find it. Where shall I call you?"

I almost told her to call me at Bogie's, but right there and then I decided to go to Packy's instead. I gave her the number and told her to call with the information.

"What are you going to do today?"

"I'll talk to some of the other P.I.s."

"Can I come along?"

"Just get me that phone number."

"What about Jenny Wheeler?"

"I haven't got a line on her yet," I said, "but I'm working on something."

"Miles—"

"I've got to go," I said, afraid that she was going to start gushing. If I could just break her of that habit she wouldn't be so annoying to talk to.

I hung up, wondering why I was bothering with her if she annoyed me so. Maybe it was because I was afraid there was a chance that Andy McWilliams *was* murdered by somebody other than the Backshooter, and if I didn't go along with Caroline nobody would ever know.

Maybe, in my present depressed state, I just wanted to make a difference.

And maybe I needed therapy.

1 1

I SPENT MOST OF the day talking to other P.I.s.

I met Henry Po at the bar he frequented called "Debbie's."
Over a beer he told me the disposition of the case he had
worked on for Andy McWilliams.

"Apparently, Andy told his client that I was handling the
case," Hank said, "because after Andy's death his client got
in touch with me."

"Did you see the case through?"

"I did, but nothing ever came of it. The guy was as clean
as a dishwasher. I can let you see the file if you like."

"I'd appreciate that," I said. "Thanks, Hank."

He promised to xerox it and have it delivered to my
apartment. I told him if I wasn't there to have it left with
the super.

As I stood up he asked, "Are you all right, Miles?"

"I'm fine. Why?"

"You seem distracted."

"No, I'm fine," I said again. "Tell me, how well did you know McWilliams?"

"We'd met once or twice."

"Any idea why he'd subcontracted a case to you?"

"You mean in particular?"

"Yes."

Hank shrugged. "No idea."

"Okay, thanks."

After leaving Po I went down to the village to Packy's bar.

"Aha, the prodigy," Packy said as I entered. His place was more on the order of a dive than Bogie's, but for a dive it was first rate.

"I think you mean prodigal," I said, climbing upon a a stool.

"Whatever," he said. "To what do I owe this honor?"

"How about a beer?"

Packy was a big ex-heavyweight who had gotten out with all of his marbles—barely—and enough money to start up his business, a bar that also served food, if you were willing to settle for cold cuts. His claim to fame was that he once went eight rounds with Rocky Marciano, before Marciano was a champ. "I coulda beat 'im," Packy always said, "If I'da had a crow bar."

He put a beer in front of me and said, "Have you stopped drinking at Bogie's?"

I picked up the beer and said, "They've started counting my drinks. Can I use your phone?"

He frowned at my remark, but didn't say anything.

"Sure," he said, and handed me the phone, which was on a twenty-five foot cord. None of those fancy cordless things for Packy.

I got Nick Delvecchio's number from information and called him in Brooklyn. As it turned out, his office and home number were the same. Just a few months ago I had tailed Nick's brother-in-law for him, and found out that he was banging a secretary he worked with during lunch. Needless to say, he was no longer related to Nick Delvecchio.

Nick was in and willing to talk about the case Caroline McWilliams had referred to him.

"The client was fairly well off," he said, without revealing the client's name, "and was afraid that her son was dealing drugs."

"How old was he?"

"Twenty."

"Was he?"

"Yes."

"Did you turn him in?"

"Yes, and his mother came, too."

"Did she want it that way?"

"She tried to get me to let him go, but—"

He didn't have to finish the sentence. Nick was an ex-cop, and simply wouldn't have been able to let a drug dealer go—not even for the boy's mother.

"How did she take it?"

"She understood," Nick said. "She was much too nice a woman to have such a monster for a son."

"What happened to the boy?"

"He's serving time."

"How far had McWilliams gotten with the case when he was killed?"

"Not very. He'd just been starting when . . . the Back-shooter got him. What's this all about, Jack?"

I told him about Caroline's suspicions, and the reasons for it.

"Kind of slim, but if I've heard right, Andy McWilliams didn't rattle easy."

"You heard right. Listen, Nick, would it be possible for you to let me see the file?"

"I don't keep real neat files, Jack, but sure, if you think it's important."

As with Hank, he promised to copy it and have it delivered. I gave him the same instructions about the super.

"All right, Nick. Thanks for the info."

"If I can help further, let me know."

"I will."

I hung up and asked Packy if I could make another call.

"As long as you're not calling Europe."

"Jersey."

He flipped his hand and said, "Go ahead."

I dialed the number and asked for Malone. It was he who answered the phone. After I explained why I was calling he was cooperative. He told me the clerk from the Meadowlands had indeed been stealing from his employers, and was now serving time, thanks to him. Malone had never met McWilliams, and had only subbed that one case for him. He had been hoping it would lead to more, but now . . .

I asked Malone if he'd let me see the file, and told him why. He said P.I.s should be like cops and go after a killer who had taken one of them out. He agreed to send me the file.

I thanked Malone for his help and hung up.

"Hot?" Packy asked.

"Cold," I said. "Speaking of which," and I pushed my empty bottle towards him. He replaced it with a full one.

I sucked on the fresh beer and knew that my next move should be to go see Walker Blue. I always hated to admit to myself that Walker intimidated me, and it was even less pleasurable in my present state of mind.

1 2

WALKER BLUE'S OFFICE WAS in a glass palace on West Fifty-seventh Street between Fifth and Sixth Avenues. I'd called first to see if he was there and his secretary had put me on hold while she checked with him to see if he was in for me. Somehow, my name did the trick. She said that he would be there for the next hour and that I could come on up.

I grabbed a cab and we worked our way through uptown traffic and got there in half an hour.

"Hi," I said to the woman behind the desk. I didn't know if she was a receptionist or his secretary. His door said WALKER BLUE INVESTIGATIONS, INC. Maybe she was part of the "Inc."

"Can I help you?" she asked, looking down her nose at me.

"Yes, I'm Miles Jacoby. I called half an hour ago and spoke to someone—"

"That was me, Mr. Jacoby," she said. She pressed her lips together for a moment, as if she'd tasted something she didn't like, and then said, "Just wait a moment, please."

When she got up I didn't bother watching her walk out. She was a matronly woman in her fifties, with graying hair worn behind her head and a very professional manner. Just the kind of woman Walker Blue would have working for him. Just the kind of woman I didn't like, and who certainly wouldn't like me. She was too stiff and formal.

She reappeared in a few moments and said, "Would you follow me, please?"

We walked down a plushy carpeted hall lined with doors to a door at the end. I wondered what was behind all those other doors. I hadn't seen Walker Blue in quite some time, and not since he'd been in this building. Blue had obviously expanded his operation, and behind some of those doors had to be some "Inc.s."

"Mr. Blue's office," she said. I assumed I was to open the door myself and enter, which I did. She closed the door behind me.

"Miles," Walker blue said from behind his huge desk. He was a tall man with an angular, long-jawed face and gray hair. "Elegant" was a word that came to mind when you saw Blue in one of his three-piece suits. Hell, I bet he'd look elegant in a sweat suit, which I also bet he'd never be caught dead in.

He stood up, but didn't come around the desk. I covered the ground between us and shook hands with him. "What can I do for you?" he asked, sitting down and motioning me to do the same.

"I'm looking into the death of Andy McWilliams, Walker," I said. I decided that since he had called me

"Miles," we must be on a first name basis. It was something
I hadn't been quite sure of up to that point.

"McWilliams?" he said, frowning. "I understood he was
killed by the Backshooter." He shook his hand and said,
"Terrible waste."

"Yes, it was, but his wife isn't so sure he was just another
random victim of the Backshooter."

He thought a moment and then said, "Caroline, right?"

"That's right."

"What does she base this belief on?"

"She says Andy was jumpy those last few weeks of his life.
How well did you know Andy, Walker?"

"Well enough to know that he didn't spook easily," he
said. "We weren't . . . friends, mind you, but we worked
together on occasion. I . . . respected his abilities."

"I need to know what the case was about that he subbed
out to you."

"You'll also want to know about the referrals."

"Yes."

"Well, the referrals weren't much," he said.

He told me about them, and he was right. One was a
missing persons case, which was still open.

"A runaway girl, sixteen," he said. "I don't see what that
could have to do with Andy's death."

The second case was a security job. A toy manufacturer
wanted McWilliams—and then Blue—to check out some
potential employees before they were hired.

"They were afraid of industrial espionage," Blue said. "I
had one of my people check them out, and we gave all but
one the okay."

"What about the one?"

"He'd been fired twice before under a cloud."

"What was his name?"

Blue frowned and asked, "Are you going to want copies of these files?"

"Yes."

He pressed a button on his intercom and asked somebody named Angel to pull the two files, make copies, and bring them to him.

"What about the third case, Walker? The one Andy subbed to you."

He made a tent out of his fingers and said, "That's a delicate matter, Miles."

"Why?"

"It involves . . . politics."

"So?"

"I'd have to check with the client on that one."

"Walker—"

He held up one hand to allay my protest. He had the longest fingers I'd ever seen. I was surprised I'd never noticed it before.

"You must trust me on this, Miles," he said. "I will check with the client and if there is no objection I will let you see the file. That is the best I can do at the moment."

I stared at him for a few moments and then said, "I guess that'll have do."

"If you stop by the outer desk on your way out you can pick up the other two files."

I stood up, started to leave, then stopped and turned back.

"Walker, you knew Andy."

He didn't say anything. It wasn't a question and he waited for me to continue.

"What would it take to make him nervous about a case?"

"Knowing Andy McWilliams's lifestyle," Walker said without hesitation, "I can't imagine what could possibly frighten him. The man wasn't even afraid of dying."

I quelled the urge to ask Walker if he was. I said thank you and left.

When I reached the front desk the woman held the files out to me.

"Are you Angel?" I asked.

She looked aghast and said, "Good heavens, no!"

She didn't seem to approve of Angel.

I found myself liking Angel, whom I hadn't even met.

$\bigtriangledown$

1 3

I DECIDED TO EAT—AND drink—somewhere I wasn't known. That let out both Bogie's and Packy's. I decided to try one of those combination Pizza Hut Express/Church's Fried Chicken places that had been popping up all over the city recently. There was one on Broadway and Fifty-first. I had chicken, fries, and biscuits, and since they also served beer, I had a few.

After I finished eating I found a bar down the block and sat in there for a while, ruminating. I was thinking about quite a few things, and my head was spinning from more than just beer.

Was I wasting my time and effort looking into this Andy McWilliams thing?" I mean, reading somebody's old reports was not only time consuming, it was boring. I had better things to do with my time, like what Heck Delgado was paying me to do—finding Two-John Wheeler.

And speaking of better things to do, I ordered another beer.

"Can I give you some advice, pal?" the bartender asked when he brought it to me. He was a typical New York bartender, which is to say he would have advice on every subject known to man. He was about my age, with slick black hair and a good set of shoulders. He could have been an ex-fighter, except his face was too smooth.

"Sure."

"A beer drunk is the worst drunk in the world. Why don't you try something else."

"Like what?"

He shrugged and said, "Bourbon, gin, scotch?"

I gave it some thought then said, "Naw, forget it. I'll stick with the beer." I hadn't been much of a drinker in the past, and had only acquired a taste for beer recently.

"Well, then, next time you're gonna drink, take some aspirin first."

"I thought that was an old wives' tale."

He shrugged again and said, "If you believe it, it'll work."

"Thanks for your concern."

After he left I went back to my morose ruminating.

This time I thought about what Willie Wells had said about a comeback. At my age—and in my condition—was that a viable alternative to what I was doing? Considering the way *that* career had ended the first time, would I be any better at it than I was at being a P.I.? That brought me back to what had happened in court last month.

"Hey, bartender!" I shouted.

"Yeah?"

"I'll try bourbon."

When I got home it was late, too late to wake the super

in my building to ask him if I'd received any special delivery packages.

At least I hadn't intended to wake him.

The next day must have been garbage day because he had a couple of trash cans in the downstairs lobby ready to go out. He usually kept them out back until morning, and then carried them to the front.

Still, if I'd been able to see straight, I probably would have been able to avoid them. As it was I walked right into them and went sprawling taking them down with me. The ensuing racket was enough to wake people on the second and third floors, not to mention the super, a Polack named Ed Koslowski.

"What the fuck—" he shouted, coming out of his apartment in his pajamas.

"Whoa, it's just me, Ed," I said, rolling over onto my back. From the way my butt felt, I was sure I'd sat in somebody's old coffee grounds.

"Jack, is that you?"

"Jesus, I just said that, didn't I?"

He hit the light switch and the lobby was bathed in bright yellow light.

"What the hell are you doing?"

"Sitting in somebody's old coffee, I think."

"Get up from there," he said, taking hold of my arm. "Look at this mess—whoa," he said backing away from me once he got me to my feet. "Whew, you're plastered! I can smell it."

"Is it that bad?" I asked, suddenly very concerned. "I'm sorry, Ed."

"Forget it," he said, looking at me funny.

"Look," I said, "look—" I slipped on a banana peel or something and he grabbed me before I could go down. "Look, let me help you clean this up."

'No, no," he said, backing away from me again, "I got it, Jack."

"I made the mess, the least I could do is help you clean it up."

"Jack," Ed said, "in your condition you wouldn't be much help. Go to bed."

"Which way is that?"

"Up one flight," he said, "and try not to trip over anything."

A lot he knows, I thought as I took the elevator up. There wasn't anything between the lobby and my apartment to trip over. Unless you counted on my own feet, of course, which somehow seemed larger and heavier than ever before.

14

I SHOULDN'T HAVE HAD the chicken fingers—at least, not with the barbecue sauce.

That's what I was thinking at six o'clock the next morning while I was hugging the porcelain throne. That bar I'd ended up in after leaving Church's Fried Chicken had chicken fingers available for its patrons, complete with choice of sauce, and at one o'clock a.m., they looked pretty good.

At six o'clock, I felt like I should have been convicted of attempted suicide.

I staggered back to my bed, feeling wrung out and tossed aside, and fell onto it on my back. When I opened my eyes the next time I was curled up like a fetus. By moving only my eyes I could see it was ten A.M.

Very cautiously I unfolded myself, prepared to bolt for the bathroom at the first sign of trouble. Once I succeeded in straightening myself out, I made a try at getting to my feet. Immediately, my stomach lurched and I made a beeline for the toilet, only to find that it was a false alarm. Actually, there was just nothing left to puke.

I turned the shower on, using only cold water, and punished myself with that for a couple of minutes. When I got out I was shivering, but I actually felt somewhat better. I dried off, pulled on a pair of jeans and a T-shirt, then had a couple of glasses of cold orange juice. I was trying to decide what to do next when somebody knocked on my door.

It was Ed Koslowski.

"Jesus, Jack, you look like shit."

"Thanks, Ed."

"What happened to you last night? You having girl trouble?"

"Yeah, Ed, girl trouble," I said. "Why are you banging on my door at such an ungodly hour?"

"What's ungodly about eleven A.M.?"

"Take my word for it."

"A couple of packages came for you by special messenger yesterday," he said, "and another one this morning." He leaned over and picked them up from the floor, where he'd set them. "I was gonna leave 'em out here, but I thought they might be important."

"Thanks, Ed," I said, taking the bundle from him. "I appreciate it."

"Listen, if you wanna tie one on again, come downstairs and drink with me. At least you know you'll get home safe."

"I'll keep that in mind, Ed. Oh, and listen, about the mess last night—"

"Forget it." Then he laughed and said, "I'm surprised you even remember. Man, you were whacked! What were you drinking?"

"I started with beer and then went to bourbon."

"Jesus, no wonder. I didn't know you hit the hard stuff. You might as well have been drinking boilermakers."

"No, never again," I said. "I'll stick to beer from now on."

"Take my advice and lighten up on that stuff, too. No broad's worth wrecking yourself over."

"I'll keep that in mind too. Thanks again, Ed."

"Sure thing."

I closed the door and deposited the bundle of envelopes on the kitchen table. I'd be able to look at them later.

I felt the beginnings of hunger in my stomach and decided to chance some toast and coffee. It went down easy enough, so I tried a second cup of coffee. After that, I started to feel like maybe I'd be able to last another day.

I opened up the packages Ed had held for me. One was from Delvecchio, another from Po, and the third—the one which had come that morning—from Malone, in Jersey. I scanned them. I didn't feel able to read them all the way through. Besides, now that I was ambulatory I had plans for the day, and they didn't include sitting inside reading reports. That I could do in the evening.

I picked up the phone and dialed a number I hadn't dialed much of late. A woman answered, and her voice triggered my memory of her. I could see her standing there, a beautiful Chinese gal with a long curtain of silky black hair, fuller breasts than you'd expect to see on a Chinese woman, and the kind of haunting face that inspired those "legends" about Chinese women.

"Hello, Lee."

"Jack," she said, as if surprised to hear my voice. I was always flattered that she never had to ask who it was when I called. "How nice to hear from you."

Tiger Lee has the most devastating telephone voice I've

ever heard, and when she uses her singsong "john" voice, the effect is doubled. With me, however, she reverts to her Brooklyn accent.

"How are you, Lee?"

"I'm fine."

"Inscrutable as ever, eh?"

She smiled—I could hear it in her voice—and said, "I wouldn't want to blow the image, you know?"

"I know."

"What can we do for you?"

"We" was she and Knock Wood Lee, her man. Wood was also Chinese, and his main source of income was his bookie operation, although he'd been known to run some girls from time to time. His real name was Nok Woo Lee.

Lee had been a hooker once, a long time ago, but not since she'd taken up with Wood. Her real name was Anna Lee. I had always thought that she might be able to change my bad luck with women for the better. Sometimes, I thought she might feel the same way.

Then again, maybe I was imagining things. Anyway, Wood was my friend.

"I'd like to come up and see Wood, Lee, if he's available."

"Always, to you.'

Wood and I had always had a working relationship, but last year he'd been arrested for murder and I'd gotten him off. Since then he'd always been accessible to me, no matter when. I think that was the reason I called on him less and less, so as not to take advantage of any debt he felt he owed me.

"When do you want to come up?"

"As soon as I can drag myself over there."

"You do sound tired."

"More than you know. I'll see you in a little while, Lee."

"I'll be counting the minutes," she said, and I could hear that smile in her voice again.

Suddenly, the day was looking a lot better.

Wood had an apartment in a building on the corner of Mott and Hester Streets, where Little Italy meets China-town. Below him was a pasta and sea food house. He owned the building and the restaurant. A block away was Um-berto's, the sight of a famous gangland rubout. He also wasn't very far from a club where I'd once visited the head of one of the New York Mafia families, Carlo Caggiano.

I took the subway to Canal Street and then walked to Wood's building. Across the street there was an Italian club, where the old men gathered to talk about old times and listen to music from the old country. I passed by the doorway to the restaurant and went to Wood's street-level door. I pressed the bell and was buzzed in. That meant that Lee had seen me from the window.

Lee opened the door, graced me with one of those smiles I'd heard on the phone, and said, "Jack, come on in."

I entered and she gave me an affectionate hug that had the same embarrassing effect on me it always had. She was tall for a Chinese woman, about five-five or so, and her full breasts pressed against me all too briefly.

"Come on, he's waiting for you."

She took my hand and led me to Wood's room, where he was sitting in his favorite chair.

"Jack, my man," he said, standing up. He was barely taller than Lee, but I knew he was proficient in several sorts of hand-to-hand combat, including karate. In fact, it had been the karate that had gotten him into trouble last year. We shook hands and he said, "Still working out?"

I knew he was talking about karate, which I had taken up

during the course of trying to clear him of the murder charge.

"I've gotten away from it, Wood."

"Sorry to hear it. Man with your athletic background—you could have made black belt fairly quickly."

"I know," I said, "I know . . . "

"Beer?"

"Sure."

"I'll get it," Lee said, leaving the room.

Wood looked around me to make sure she was gone, then said, "What's wrong with you?"

"What do you mean?"

"You look like shit," he said.

"I've been told that—"

"I'm not kidding," he said. "You getting enough sleep? Having trouble with a woman?"

"I've just been busy, Wood."

"Maybe you could use a good woman? I'll guarantee she's clean—"

"No, thanks. Maybe another time."

He shrugged and sat in his chair.

"What can I do for you then?"

"I've been looking for Two-John Wheeler for the better part of a week now. You know her?"

"I know her."

"So do I," Lee said, reentering the room with two bottles of Dos Equis beer.

She handed them to us while giving me a reproachful look. "Stay away from Jenny Wheeler, Jack. You could catch something just by looking at her."

"Lee!" Woods said, scolding her.

"Well, he could," she said, defending herself.

She walked over to his chair, sat on the arm, took his bottle, and had a sip. I found myself wishing she had taken a sip from mine instead. I had tasted her lips before, but only in the most chaste fashion. I envied Wood.

"Why do you want Two-John?" Wood asked.

"Heck Delgado wants her."

Heck had been ready to defend Wood against the murder charge until I'd found the evidence that got him off.

"That's good enough for me then."

"You know where she is?'"

"No, but I will," he said. "Just give me a couple of days."

"She doesn't want to be found," I warned him.

"That might make it a little harder," he said, "but we'll see. I'll call you as soon as I know something."

"I appreciate it."

I stood up and Lee lifted her gorgeous butt of the arm of his chair. She took my arm and started to walk me to the door. I stopped abruptly and turned to face Wood again.

"One more thing."

"Name it."

"You know a street punk named Binky?"

Wood made a face and said, "I know him. You've got to acquire a better class of snitch."

"See if you can locate him for me, will you? He gave me a line on Two-John, but it was a little late."

"You going to give him another chance?"

"I'd like to talk to him about the last one."

"I'll see what I can do."

I went out into the hall with Lee.

"Tell me something," she said, when we were out of Wood's earshot.

"What?"

"What's wrong?"

"What is it, written on my face?" I asked, a bit testily.

"To your friends, yes," she said.

"Things just haven't been going very well, Lee, that's all. They'll pick up."

She stared at me for a long moment and then said, "Well, I hope so. Just remember what I said about Two-John, Jack. She's good-looking, but stay away from her."

"After seeing you, how could I ever consider another woman?" I said.

"You're sweet."

I handed her the half-empty beer bottle and she took a drink from it. As I went out the door I entertained the thought of asking for the bottle back.

15

I THOUGHT ABOUT GOING to Bogie's for lunch but I didn't want to listen to Billy or Stuart lecture me again about the dangers of demon rum. Besides, I still had some beer in the refrigerator.

I stopped at the deli across the street for a turkey breast hero, thinking about what Willy had said about losing weight. Turkey was less fattening than roast beer.

I put Caroline's reports on the table, intending to read them while I ate. Instead, I gave my attention to devouring the sandwich and two quick beers. I was popping the tab on the third one when the phone rang.

I wiped my hands on a napkin and picked up the phone. "Hello."

"Miles, it's Caroline. I've been looking for you."

"Well, you found me."

There was a long silence and then she said, "I haven't

heard from you since yesterday morning."

"I haven't had anything to tell you."

"Did you talk to the others? I mean, the other investigators—"

"I did. I'm looking at their files now."

"And?"

"And nothing, Caroline," I said. "I'm still looking at them. I've just finished having lunch and right now I'm going to have another beer."

"Jack—"

"Look, Caroline," I said, "no matter who I work for, I don't do daily reports. Now, I'm looking over the files that I have, and I've put the word out to friends of mine about Two-John. I'm also waiting for some information from a cop I know who's working on the Backshooter task force. There's not much else I can do."

"All right," she said, 'I . . . I'll wait for you to call me."

"Yeah, you do that."

I'd started to hang up when she said, "Miles?"

"What?"

"I know I'm not very good at . . . at running an office, but I'm a very good cook. Would you, uh, like me to make you dinner tonight?"

"Dinner?"

"I really am a very good cook."

"Sure, Caroline," I said. "Why not?"

I agreed to be at her apartment at seven P.M., and we hung up.

I was about to sit down when the phone rang again.

"Jack? It's Hocus."

"What's up?"

"Stilwell wants to meet with you. He says he has what you asked for."

"Does he want a meal again?"

"No. He said he'd settle for a drink this time, someplace out of the way."

"Let me think a minute," I said, but it didn't take that long. I gave him Packy's address and told him to have Stilwell meet me there at eleven P.M.

"You getting anywhere on the Andy McWilliams thing?" Hocus asked.

"Not very far. Why?"

"Curious, that's all," Hocus said.

"Cops don't get curious for no reason, Hocus."

"Cops are people, Jack."

"No! Who told you that?"

"My mother."

"Was she a cop?"

"No, but she was married to one."

"Mothers are people, too, Hocus."

"What's that mean?"

"It means that people fib."

"Not my mother," he said. "I'll be talking to you."

I spent the rest of the afternoon in my apartment, going over reports, waiting for a call from Wood, or Binky, or Walker Blue—or someone! I wanted somebody to call me and give me all the answers, but it probably never would happen.

At six I quit reading and showered. I hadn't seen anything in the reports that would explain why Andy McWilliams was jumpy the last weeks of his life. I could only hope that Walker Blue would get his client's permission to reveal his file to me, and that there would be something there. I also hoped that whatever Stilwell had for me and whatever Wood could dig up would all add up to something that would help.

At six-thirty I left my apartment and went out to find a cab. I wondered if I had done the right thing in accepting Caroline's invitation for dinner. I also wondered why she had invited me. She was a lovely woman and had been alone for the past five months. I wondered if she'd been with a man during that time, then I wondered what Alison was doing tonight. Or Julie. Jesus, why did I think of Julie?

$\bigtriangledown$

1 6

THE CAB DROPPED ME on Eighty-second and York at 6:55. At 7:05 I was being let into the apartment by Caroline.

"You have a very slow elevator," I said. "And a very small one." It would barely have accommodated three normal-sized people.

"I forgive you for being five minutes late."

I should have known something was up when I saw the way she was dressed. It didn't dawn on me then that she was striving for what women usually strive for when they dress, to look good—and she certainly did that. She was wearing blue jeans and an off-the-shoulder blouse that showed-off her rounded shoulders and smooth skin. Her hair hung loosely about her shoulders and I detected a subtle scent of perfume that was quite pleasant. I wondered why I hadn't noticed before that she bore a strong resemblance to the actress Jennifer O'Neill.

For the first time since she had walked into Bogie's I realized what a looker she was.

"Can I take your jacket?" she asked.

"Oh, sure."

She opened a closet door in the entry hall and hung up my jacket, then led me into the apartment. I could see a dining room and living room. I assumed that there was also a kitchen, which must have been where the good smells were coming from. There was a hallway with two doorways, one of which must have led to a bedroom. The decor was modern, and oddly cold. The place was neat as a pin, unlike the office. I guessed that she was a good housekeeper when there was no paperwork involved.

"We were never much for decorating."

"It looks fine. What's that I smell?"

"Dinner," she said. "Come with me while I check it and I'll get you a beer."

"Lead the way."

On the other side of the dining room was another hall, which led to the kitchen. There was also another door to the hallway there, which was bolted shut.

In the kitchen she opened the refrigerator and pulled out a Paulie Girl.

"I hope you didn't buy that just for me," I said, accepting it.

"As a matter of fact, I did," she said. "A six pack."

"Well . . . thank you."

Damned if I wasn't nervous. I had never expected to find myself in a social situation with her, and I wasn't quite sure how to act.

"Do you like chicken?" she asked, opening the oven.

"Yes."

"Good, I've made a lemon chicken. It's a speciality of mine."

From the way the chicken looked it was obvious to me that she was a good cook. Perhaps what she had said was true and it was only detective work that she was unable to cope with effectively. She seemed in control of other aspects of life.

"It smells wonderful."

"I've made some broccoli and candied yams to go with it, and a salad."

"It all sounds very good."

She closed the door to the oven and turned to face me.

"Do you cook?"

"I usually eat out, or bring something in."

"Then you'll enjoy a good home-cooked meal."

"I'm sure I will."

She studied me for a moment and then asked, "Are you nervous?"

"Yes."

"So am I," she said. "It's silly, isn't it?"

"Very," I said.

Just admitting it to each other seemed to take some of the pressure off.

"Let me get a glass of white wine and we'll go and sit in the living room. Dinner will be ready in about twenty minutes."

"Fine."

Even with some of the tension removed, the chatter was inane and continued in that fashion. At one point she said, "I don't really know what to call you. Should I call you Miles?'

'If you like," I said. "Some people call me Miles, some call me Jack. Whichever you feel most comfortable with is all right with me."

"I like Miles," she said, pausing as if to roll it around on her tongue. I found the thought more than a bit erotic. "Yes," she said, "Miles."

"Has anyone ever called you . . . Carrie?" I asked, and she gave me a dirty look and said not if they cared about their health.

The meal itself was as she had promised, a *very* good home-cooked meal.

"Some coffee?" she asked, as she cleared the table of plates."

"Yes, thanks. Caroline?"

"Yes?" I'd stopped her progress towards the kitchen.

"Did Andy have an office here?"

"Yes, he did. It's the first door on the left, down that hall."

Still another hall, at the end of which was the bathroom. The first door was the office and the second must have been the bedroom.

"Would you mind if I had a look around the office?"

"No, go ahead. I'll get the coffee."

She went into the kitchen while I walked down the hall to Andy's office. It was simple—just a desk, a couple of file cabinets, and some bookshelves. I went around behind the desk and sat down. On my left, sitting on a wing of the desk, was a Panasonic electronic typewriter. On the desk was one of those phones that has a couple of rows of buttons. You program each button for a phone number, so that when you went to call that number, you only have to press one button. I leaned over and saw that each button was marked with some sort of abbreviation or a name.

There was a button marked "Blue," for Walker Blue, no doubt. One marked "office," which I assumed was for his own office. There were others marked, "P.D.," "DMV," "Con Ed," and others that were obvious. Then there were the short names—"Bob," "Sam," 'Ed," "Don,"—either

friends or contacts of some sort. As Caroline entered the
room with a tray I saw a button labelled "Tower," and
wondered why that was.

"Don't get up," she said.

She put the tray on the desk and poured two cups of coffee
from the pot. She sat in the chair facing the desk. I picked
up the cup she'd poured for me and sat back.

"Do you know what all these buttons are for?"

"Some of them," she said. "Not all. In fact, not many.
The one marked *office* is for his office, and some of the others
are obvious."

"Sure," I said. "Motor Vehicle and Con Edison. Is the one
marked *P.D. 911*, a precinct, or a police contact?"

"I'm not sure."

"Do you mind if I go through those cabinets?"

"No. They're mostly closed out cases, though."

"I'll just leaf through them."

I put the coffee down and walked over to one of the
cabinets. They were built into a wall unit with bookshelves,
and they opened by lifting the door up and then sliding it in.
Rather than running front to back, the files ran left to right
on a drawer that slid out on rollers.

Caroline remained seated and quiet as I leafed through the
folders. She was right—they were closed cases, but I found
some of the client names on them interesting, even impressive.

I closed the first drawer, opened the second, and found
more of the same. Finally, I closed the drawer and began
examining the books on the shelves.

"I don't believe it," I said, pulling one out. It was something called *The Burning Season* by Wayne Dundee. I held
the book in my hands and read off some of the other author
names. "Chandler, Spillane, Ross Macdonald, Bill Pronzini.
Are they all detective novels?"

"Most of them. It was a passion with him. He said none of them were realistic, but he enjoyed reading them, and had since he was a boy. It's why he became a private investigator."

I slid the Dundee book back into place somewhere between Chandler and Estleman. I would never have suspected that Andy McWilliams was a mystery fan, but he probably had lots of quirks I didn't know about, I thought, recalling his behavior at that convention I'd attended, the one where he'd had a blonde on his arm.

I turned and looked at Caroline, who was just sitting there with her legs crossed, watching me, and wondered what he'd needed with a flashy blonde.

"How about a glass of brandy?" she asked.

"Sounds good."

She left and I went back behind the desk and sat down. My eyes strayed to the phone again, and that button marked, "Tower." Was it a name, or a place?

She came in with two snifters of brandy and handed me one, then she sat down and we stared at each other a while.

"You know," she said, "Andy's been dead more than five months."

I didn't say anything.

"In all that time I haven't . . . haven't seen anyone."

I didn't know what she wanted me to say, but I thought about the off-the-shoulder blouse she was wearing.

"Mourning periods used to be longer than they are now," she continued, "and people have needs—"

"What are you trying to say, Caroline?"

She looked at me steadily and said, "I'd like you to stay tonight, Miles."

I put the brandy down on the desk. Aside from the obvious drawbacks to casual sex—AIDS being no small part of them—it just didn't seem like a good idea to me. Of course,

I *was* attracted to her, but we just hadn't known each other very long.

"I don't think it's a good idea, Caroline."

"This isn't casual, Miles," she said. "I mean, I haven't even been attracted to a man since Andy's death."

"I appreciate that—"

"If your worried for . . . for health reasons, I can assure you—"

I looked at my watch and saw that it was nearly ten o'clock.

"I've got to meet a man tonight, Caroline," I said. "A cop who I hope will have something to tell me about Andy's death."

"Oh, I see," she said, lowering her eyes. "That's the reason." She looked at me and said, "What about after—"

"Caroline—"

"I'm sorry," she said, "I don't mean to push you. Are you involved with someone?"

"Not at the moment."

"That what is it?"

"I just think we should . . . know each other a little better before . . . before we consider anything. I also think we should get this case out of the way first.'

She studied me for a few moments then said, "You're an odd man, Miles."

"Not really," I said, standing up. "I'd better get a move on if I'm going to make my meeting."

She stood also and walked me out to the door.

"Will you call me if you find out anything important?"

"I'll call you."

She leaned into me, making contact chest to chest and kissed me. I don't know if she meant to kiss my mouth or my cheek, but she got the corner of my mouth.

"Thanks."

I nodded and said, "I'll call you," and got out of there before my resolve failed me.

17

$\triangledown$

WHEN I GOT TO Packy's place Stilwell was already there, sitting at the bar. He was dressed much as he had been when we'd had dinner uptown, but the difference was that down here at Packy's he fit right in with the rest of the clientele.

I slid onto a stool next to him and said, "Got a drink already?"

"A couple," he said, looking at me. "Looks like you've had a couple, too."

"Never mind." I'd had some beer at Caroline's, and a glass of brandy. So what? I was still pretty steady.

"I told the big fella that the drinks were on you," he said. "Okay?"

"Fine," I said, and waved to Packy, who came over.

"This fella a friend of yours, Jack?"

"Yeah, Packy, I guess you could call him that. Got a beer for me?"

"Always," he said. He pulled out a bottle of Rolling Rock and set it in front of me.

"What's this?" I asked, picking up the cold, sweaty green bottle.

"Ordered a case to see how it is."

"I'm the guinea pig?"

"Yup."

I'd had Rolling Rock before and it was okay, but I humored Packy and said, "Okay, let me work on it." Before he left I said to Stilwell, "You still good?"

He raised his half-filled glass and said, "I'm just fine."

"Okay," I said, after Packy had gone down to the other end of the bar to talk boxing with three other customers, "what did you find out?"

"You wanted to know what caliber bullet Andy McWilliams was killed with, right?"

"Right."

"He was killed with the nine millimeter."

"That's an odd gun for someone to be carrying around, isn't it?"

"It's more out of the ordinary than the others, sure," Stilwell said. "That doesn't mean he *wasn't* killed by the Backshooter."

"It doesn't mean he was either."

"Well,' Stilwell said, "I just hope this helps you."

"I hope so too," I said, taking a long pull on the Rolling Rock.

"That any good?" he asked.

"Yeah, it's okay."

"Well," he said, "I've got to get going."

I put my hand on his arm and said, "Did you come up with anything else?"

"What else is there?" he asked. "The killing fits in with the others."

"I know, I know," I said, taking my hand from his arm. "Thanks for your help, Steve."

"I just hope it does something for you eventually."

"Yeah, so do I."

Stilwell left and Packy came down the bar.

"How is that?" he asked.

"It's okay," I said.

"Just okay."

"Yeah, what do you want, Packy? It's okay."

"Okay," he said, holding his hand up in front of him. "So it's okay, so you wouldn't do no TV commercial for it. Give it back and I'll give you something else."

"No," I said, "its okay—I mean, it's all right. I'll drink it. Look," I said, slowing myself down, "I'm sorry, I didn't mean to snap at you."

"You having girl trouble, Jack?"

"Yeah," I said, so I wouldn't have to explain further to him, "I'm having girl trouble, Packy."

"Well," he said, shrugging his big, sloping shoulders, "that's one thing I can't help you with, so I'll leave you alone."

"Okay, Pack," I said. "I appreciate it."

He started to walk away, then turned back and said, "Oh, I got a message for you."

"From who?"

"I wrote it down," he said. He popped the drawer on the register and took out a piece of paper.

"'Call Wood,' it says. You know what that means?"

"I know," I said. "Gimme the phone." He handed me the phone and I asked. "When did you get this message?"

"I dunno," he said, "maybe a couple of hours ago. Come to think of it, he said he'd been looking for you."

"Great," I said, dialing. He probably had a line on Two-

John, and I was busy having dinner and playing footsie with Caroline.

"Hello?" Lee said, answering.

"Lee, it's Jack."

"I know."

"I hope I'm not calling too late. Is Wood there?"

"Hold on."

I waited a few seconds and then Wood came on the phone.

"Where you been, my man?" he asked. "I've been trying to track you all night."

"I was indisposed," I said. "What have you got?"

"A location on Jenny Wheeler."

"Great! Shoot!"

"She's holed up in a dive on Forty-third and Eighth," he said.

"Got a room number?"

"Of course," he said, his tone reproaching me. "415."

"Is she there now?"

"She was yesterday," he said. "I can't say for sure that she's there now. That's up to you to find out."

"So I will," I said. "Thanks for this, Wood."

"Keep me posted," he said. "If she's not there, I'll keep looking."

I hung up, thought a moment, then dialed Heck's office. I knew he wouldn't be there, but his machine was on and I left a message about Jenny's possible location and told him I'd call him in the morning.

"What another beer?" Packy asked when I handed back the phone.

"No thanks, Pack," I said, sliding off the stool. "I've got to pay a long-overdue visit." I tossed some money on the bar and hurried out, hoping that this time Town-John would still be there when I got there.

Wood was right. In fact, the place on Forty-third and Eighth wasn't even good enough to be called a "dive." This made the place in Alphabet City look like the Sheraton.

After leaving Packy's it had taken me all of twenty minutes to get a cab. They're anything but a dime a dozen in the Village after midnight.

I went into the lobby and the guy behind the desk didn't budge. As I moved towards the elevator I heard him start to snore. The elevator was even smaller then the one in Caroline's building and I got in and tried a few buttons before I realized it wasn't working.

I started up the stairs and passed a hooker and her john on the way down. The guy kept going as she stopped on the stairs next to me.

"Looking for somebody special, honey?" she asked. There might have been some time in her life when she'd looked good, but this wasn't it.

"Vice, honey," I said, wanting to send her on her way.

"Ooh, baby," she said, smiling lasciviously, "you'll find plenty of that here," and went on her way, cackling.

I climbed the stairs to the fourth floor without encountering anyone else and groped my way down the darkened hallway to room 415.

I knocked on the door and put my ear to it. I was hoping that if she tried to go out the window I'd be able to hear her. When there was no answer I knocked again.

This time when there was no answer I tried the doorknob. Even before I turned it the door opened. I saw that the lock had been broken sometime and had not been fixed.

"Oh, Jenny," I said, "if you were looking for someplace safe and secure, you came to the wrong place."

Already convinced that she was gone I pushed the door open and entered anyway.

I smelled it even before I turned the light on.

I groped around on the wall for the switch, breathing shallowly. It's amazing how much copper you can smell when there's a lot of blood. You can even taste it in your mouth, brackish and sour.

I found the switch and as I turned it on I steeled myself for what I would see.

The light went on, bathing the room in a dim, yellow glow, but it was enough.

There was a bed and a dresser, a sink and chair, and not much else.

Not much, that is, except for Two-John Wheeler.

She was on the bed, head at the foot. Blood from her throat had soaked through the sheets around her head and was now leaking onto the floor. The blood hadn't had time to soak into the rest of sheets, which told me she'd been killed recently.

Very recently.

Like while I was fucking around looking for a goddamned cab!

18

I WAITED OUT IN the hall while the detectives and lab boys did their thing. Pretty soon the M.E. arrived, and I recognized him as Dr. Mahbee. Hocus like to drive him crazy by calling him Dr. "Maybe." He was a handsome West Indian who was usually all business.

He stopped just outside the room and stared at me.

"I know you, don't I?"

"Jacoby," I said.

"Oh, yes, the private investigator," he said, and went inside.

I had called 911 because I knew Hocus wouldn't be on duty. Whoever had the nightwatch could respond, and as it turned out there was one detective I knew and one I didn't.

When they arrived I met them in the lobby and showed them to the room. They went in, and soon after the lab fellas arrived. Now that the M.E. had gone in, one of the detectives came out to talk to me. He was the one I knew, a guy named Names, Detective Larry Names. He worked out of the Seventeenth. "Tell me about it," he said.

I gave it to him in a nutshell, about how I was looking for Jenny Wheeler and had gotten a tip that she was here.

"From who?"

"From a voice on the phone," I said. After all, that wasn't a lie, was it?

"Okay, go ahead."

I told him that the clerk was asleep when I arrived, and that I went upstairs and let myself in.

"You do the lock?"

"No," I said, "it was like that. I figured most of them in this place were like that."

"It's been kicked in recently," he said, fingering the splintered wood around the lock.

"By the killer."

"More than likely," he said, agreeing. "You see anybody?"

"I passed a hooker on the stairs."

"You sure she was a hooker?"

"I know a hooker when I see one, Names."

"Don't get testy," he said. "I know you, but we ain't friends. You got it?"

"I got it."

"Give me anything else you've got," he said. "I got to write it up for the homicide boys."

"That's it," I said, "the whole ball o' wax."

He studied me for a few minutes and then said, "Okay. We've got to wait for the Duty Captain to show up, and then we'll be going to the precinct. This is gonna be a long night, so get ready."

"I'm ready."

He stared at me for a moment and then said, "You drunk?"

"I was—a little—when I got here," I said.

"Yeah," he said, 'yeah, I can see how this might sober you up." He reached into his pocket and took out a package of gum. "Here, have a few of these. The Captain's a hard-on and if he smells you, he'll give you a hard time."

"Thanks," I said, taking it. I unwrapped two pieces and popped them into my mouth just as a man in uniform with captain's bars showed up.

"You a cop?" he demanded.

"Nope."

He charged into the room bellowing, "What the hell is this civilian doing here?"

Names was right. It was a real long night.

It was light out when I got home. I wasn't drunk anymore, but I wanted to be. My eyes were gritty and my mouth tasted like shit. And I felt like shit too, because I had been having a nice dinner and some drinks while Two-John Wheeler was having her throat cut.

That was worth getting drunk about, wasn't it? Only I was too tired to do anything but fall into bed. I'd get drunk later.

$\bigtriangledown$

1 9

I WOKE THE NEXT MORNING without that familiar hungover feeling.

Actually it wasn't the next morning, it was afternoon. Once I realized that, I remembered what happened the night before, and what had kept me out until early morning.

I got out of bed and put on a pot of coffee, then sat down to evaluate the situation.

Technically speaking, with Two-John dead my job for Heck was finished. I'd found her, she was dead, and now he'd have to figure out some other way to help his client.

With Two-John dead—and again being technical—I was also finished with Caroline McWilliams. There was no way to ask Two-John what she knew about Andy's death.

And so—again dealing technically—I was now unemployed—except for one thing. I wanted to know who killed Two-John, and how they had gotten to her ahead of me.

Obviously, someone else had been looking for her and had twice beat me there, but who was it?

I called Caroline's apartment, and when she didn't answer I tried her office.

"Hello," she said. "I just thought I'd . . . keep busy, you know?"

"Sure, I understand," I said. "I have some bad news, Caroline."

"About Andy?"

"Not exactly."

I told her about my lead on Two-John, and what I found when I got there.

"She's dead?"

"I'm afraid so."

"But that . . . puts us at a dead end."

"Yes."

"Well . . . you're not going to quit, are you, Miles?"

"Caroline," I said, "I spent the whole night with the cops. Let's talk about this when I'm a little more alert, all right?"

"Soon?" she asked hopefully.

"I'll call you," I said. "I promise."

After we hung up I called Heck Delgado's office.

"Law Office," Missy's voice answered.

"Missy, it's Jack. Is he in?"

"Yes, but he's got to leave in five minutes."

"That's all I need."

"I'll get him."

After a moment Heck came on the line.

"I got your message," he said. "Did you find her?"

"Yes."

"Good."

"Dead."

"Oh . . . how?"

"Her throat was cut."

"Who did it?"

"Don't know," I said. "I spent the whole night with the detectives. They'll have an autopsy report later today, but her throat was definitely cut. I don't think they'll find anything else."

"Well, that's that then."

"I'm sorry I didn't get to her in time," I said. "I feel guilty about that."

"Jesus, that's just what you need, something else to feel guilty about."

"Yeah, I know."

"Send me a bill, Miles, and I'll send you a check."

"I don't feel like I earned—"

"My client can afford it."

"Your client—" I said, "Scalesi."

"Right."

"Hmm . . ."

"What's that mean?"

"Did Scalesi know Two-John?"

"That's privileged information, Miles," Heck said. "I'd have to get permission to answer a question like that."

"Could you get me an appointment with him?"

"Again, I could only ask him."

"Would you do that and get back to me?"

"Sure."

"If I'm not here leave a message with . . . with Caroline McWilliams." I gave him her office and home numbers.

"Correct me if I'm wrong, but with Jenny Wheeler dead, you association with the lady should be over, shouldn't it?"

"Yes," I said, "it should," and I did not elaborate.

"All right," Heck said after a moment of silence. "I'll see

what I can do. I hung up and still had my hand on the phone when it rang. I snatched it up.

"Hello?"

"Jacoby?"

I recognized the voice just from that one word. It was Walker Blue.

"Yes, Walker?"

"I've been trying to get ahold of you," he said. He sounded annoyed.

"I've been busy."

"You should get an answering machine or a secretary."

"I've been thinking about it," I said, rubbing my eyes with the thumb and forefinger of my left hand.

"You wanted information on that subcontracted case I took from Andy McWilliams."

"Yes," I said, then dropped my hand away from my eyes and said, "Yes," again, with more enthusiasm. "Do you have it?"

"Not exactly."

"What does that mean?"

"I did not get the okay to show you the file, but the client would like to see you."

"Okay," I said, "that's just as good."

"Take down his name and address."

I groped around for something to write on and pulled over a two-day-old *New York Post* and a pencil.

"Go ahead."

"His name is Jules Van Voorhies—"

"Say that again?"

"I will spell it," he said, patiently. "He is Dutch."

"I see. And his address?"

"He has an office in the Trump Tower."

I didn't bother writing that down.

After I hung up I replayed the last part of the conversation in my mind.

"There is something I should tell you."

"What's that?"

"I did not complete the job."

"Why not."

There was a pause and then he said, "I did not like the man."

Blue wouldn't elaborate. He simply told me I should call Van Voorhies and make an appointment.

I started to get up with the intention of taking a shower when the phone rang again.

"Yeah?"

"Cheery this morning, aren't we?" Knock Wood Lee said.

"No," I said, and explained why.

"Jeez, I'm sorry, Jack."

"It wasn't your fault," I said. "If you'd been able to find me sooner, the girl would still be alive."

"Well, don't go taking the blame yourself," he said.

"No," I said, "I'll find someone to share it with—like the killer."

"That's the cops' job."

"With me," I said, "it's not a job."

He told me to be careful and to call if I needed help. I asked him to keep looking for Binky, and we hung up.

I meant to run to the shower before the phone could ring again, but I didn't make it.

I meant to say, "What the fuck!" and then pick up the phone, but in my haste I did it backwards, and the calling party got an earful.

"Jacoby? Is that you?" Hocus asked.

"Jesus—yeah, Hocus, I'm sorry," I said. "I had a helluva night."

"I heard," he said. "I wish I didn't have to bother you with this, I really do."

He sounded deadly serious.

"What's the matter?"

"It's your friend, Packy."

"Packy?" I said, puzzled. "What's wrong? Did something happen to him?"

"Yeah, something happened to him," Hocus said. "Jesus, I'm sorry, Jack, but he's dead."

"He—what?"

"He's dead, Jack."

"Packy?" I asked, stunned. I fell into a kitchen chair and leaned on the table. "Packy? Are you sure?"

"I'm sure, Jack."

"What happened?"

"He was shot," Hocus, "in the back."

"In that back?"

"Yeah," Hocus said. "The Backshooter, Jack. They think the Backshooter got him."

20

WHEN THE SON OF Sam—otherwise known as the .44 Caliber Killer—was running around New York shooting people, I often wondered how it would feel if he got someone I knew. I was a lot younger then.

Now I knew what it would have felt like. Shitty!

I had been to the morgue to see Packy. It was something I felt I had to do—to say good bye, I guess. Also, he had no family, so I identified him. After leaving the morgue I went to Hocus's office. It wasn't his case, but we were friends and he had gotten me all the particulars.

"Apparently," he said, looking across his desk at me with sympathetic eyes, "the fucker got him while he was walking home."

"In the back?"

"Yes."

"And the playing card, as well?"

"Yes."

"Damn!"

The medical examiner said that Packy had been killed somewhere between three A.M.—when he closed—and four A.M. He'd been dragged into an alley and thrown into some garbage. The garbage men found him around seven. More than likely he was killed shortly after three, while he was walking home."

"How did he choose Packy?" I asked angrily.

"Who knows?"

"Maybe the fucker even had a drink in his place."

"Jack—"

I shook my head and suddenly tears formed in my eyes. I squeezed my eyes shut, forcing the tears down my cheeks, but holding back others.

"Jesus," I said, "Packy was harmless. Even when he was a fighter he was harmless outside the ring. He was the original gentle giant."

Big and strong as Packy was, he was even gentle *inside* the ring, which was why he never got past being a prelim fighter. I hadn't known him when he was fighting—I only met him when he opened his place. Even though he was older, we became friends because we had been through many of the same things.

"I wonder."

"What?"

"What?" I said. I hadn't been aware that I had said anything loud enough for Hocus to hear.

"What do you wonder?"

"I wonder if Packy ever really fought Marciano."

Hocus shrugged.

"You could look it up."

"Nah," I said, "I won't."

"Did he have any family?"

"Nobody," I said, "not a one. His parents are dead, and he had no brothers, no sisters, and no cousins."

"If you want I can get you his personal effects."

"Sure," I said. "Thanks. I'd appreciate it. Will I be able to go inside his place?"

"I don't see why not," Hocus said. "He was killed outside, and the keys are probably among his things. What do you plan to do?"

"Find the name of his lawyer or his accountants, I guess" I said. "Somebody's got to take care of his place."

"They'll probably sell it," he said, "unless he's got a will."

"I guess. I don't know . . . "

"Wait here," he said. "Let me go up to the task force and see what I can find out. Maybe I can get you his things now."

"I appreciate it."

"I may have to tell a white lie," he said.

"Like?"

"Like you're his brother, or something."

"Cousin," I said. "Make me his cousin. I've already lost one brother.

"Oh," Hocus said, "yeah, right. Okay, cousin, just sit tight."

I tried to sit tight, but more than anything, I wanted a drink. After fifteen minutes I'd had enough. I left Hocus a note that I'd be in a bar a couple of blocks away, one I knew the cops used, and told him to meet me there.

I went to get my drink.

The bar was on Fiftieth, between Second and Third Avenues. By the time Hocus arrived, I was well into my third drink.

He slid onto a stool next to me and the bartender came over.

"Hocus-Pocus," he said. "This fella is a friend of yours?"

"I guess you could call him that," Hocus said, "Why?"

"He's gone through three bourbons in record time."

Hocus poked me and said, "I didn't know you drank hard liquor."

"I don't," I said, finishing my third drink. "Give me another," I said to the bartender.

"Bring him a cup of coffee," Hocus said.

"I don't want coffee," I said thickly.

"Your friend is dead, Jack," Hocus said. "Getting fucked up isn't gonna bring him back."

I didn't have an answer for that.

"Besides, you've been drinking a lot lately, haven't you?"

"Who told you that lie?"

"Stilwell," Hocus said. "He said he had to put you in a cab that night you had dinner together."

"So," I said, "that once."

"He also said you were half in the bag when you got there."

The bartender came with the coffee and I glared at him. He looked at Hocus, and then walked away, leaving the cup of steaming hot black coffee in front of me.

"What started you off?" he asked. "Not that bullshit with Dicky last month?"

I looked at him and I guess he could see the guilt in my face.

"Jesus, Jack," he said, "if you're gonna turn into a drunk, do it for a better reason than that."

I expected him to go on about it, but surprisingly he dropped it after that.

"I brought this stuff for you," he said, putting an eight by ten manila envelope on the bar. It was bulging from the contents.

"What's in it?"

"Wallet, watch, some change, keys—I assume they key to his place will be in there."

"Yeah, I guess," I said. For want of something better to do with my hands I picked up the coffee cup and had a sip.

Hocus looked at his watch and said, "I've got to go, Jack."

"Hocus, are they sure?" I asked as he got off his stool. "Are they sure he was killed by the Backshooter?"

He clapped me on the shoulder and said, "As sure as they've been about any of the others."

As Hocus went out the door the bartender came back and said, "You gonna finish that?" indicating the coffee.

"No," I said, "it tastes like shit."

"This is a bar," he said, "not a coffee shop. I suppose you want another drink?"

"Yeah," I said, picking up the envelope and sliding off my stool, "I do, but I know a better place to get it."

$\triangledown$

21

I WENT TO PACKY'S. Using his keys I opened the back door—having to go through four keys before I found the right one—and went inside. I turned on the light and found myself in Packy's back room, which he used for both storage and office space. There were racks of shelves against two walls, well stocked with booze. Up against a third there was an old wooden desk, pitted and scarred. The overhead light was dim so I turned on the desk lamp. It was one I had bought for him after I'd been back here one time and saw how dark it was. The flourescent bulb winked a couple of times, then caught and flashed on, bathing the desk top in white light.

I sat down and began going through the desk.

When I had the desk top covered with papers and ledgers I realized I was thirsty. I went through the small kitchen into the main room and came out behind the bar. I grabbed a glass, surveyed the bottles of hard liquor on the shelf and behind the bar, then bent down and opened the cooler. I reached for a bottle of Bud, then saw the green Rolling Rock bottles and took one. I replaced the glass and went into the back room with the cold beer.

I nursed the beer while I went through Packy's papers. Something Hocus said to me earlier had hit home, about becoming a drunk for a good reason. In light of everything that had happened recently—both Jenny Wheeler and Packy being killed—having been humiliated by that pissant Dicky Hilary didn't seem reason enough.

Not anymore.

When I left Packy's place I knew who his accountant was and who his lawyer was. I also knew something else. I had found a newspaper clipping, which I folded up and put in my wallet. It was yellowed with age and was a report of the fight between two up-and-coming heavyweights named Packy Moran and Rocky Marciano. Marciano had won by a knockout.

Packy really had fought Rocky Marciano!

I locked the place up tight and stood for a moment in the now darkened alley.

What had Packy thought that last moment, I wondered? What had he felt or heard? The scrape of a shoe? The sound of a hammer being cocked? Had he heard the report of the gun, or felt the impact of the bullet?

What did Packy know about guns? He probably had no idea what was happening to him. Maybe he had lain with his face pressed to the cold ground, wondering what the hell was going on. I hoped not. I hoped he had died quickly.

I picked up a roast beef sandwich at the deli across the street and took it up to my apartment. The smile the girl behind the counter gave me didn't do anything for me, but that wasn't her fault.

It was nine P.M. I took a bite. It was a good sandwich, but I wasn't really in the mood. What I wanted was a drink. I went to the refrigerator and looked at the two cans of Meister Brau that were left, and then closed the door.

Maybe I needed some company. Who should I call? If I was an alcoholic and a member of AA, at least I'd have a list of names to call if I felt like a drink. It's in moments like this that people discover how many friends they really have. I could only think of one person to call. Alison.

$\triangledown$

22

W<small>E ATE IN BED.</small>

Alison had brought some cold cuts with her, bread, a one liter bottle of cream soda, and a pound of German potato salad. She knew I loved the stuff.

When I answered the door she had thrown her arms around me and hugged me tightly. It was what I needed, and it was all I could do to keep me from crying. After a moment she had backed away and handed me a bag.

"What's this?"

"German potato salad."

"Great."

"You want to eat first?" she had asked, closing my door, "or go to bed?"

"Oh," I had said, "bed, definitely."

For a little while, I had lost myself in the smoothness and warmth of her skin, the sweetness of her mouth, the fragrance of her hair, forgetting everything and everyone else . . .

Afterward she constructed a couple of impressive sand-wiches and returned to bed with them, the potato salad, a couple of plastic forks, and the bottle of soda. We ate and passed the soda bottle back and forth, drinking from it and laughing. And then we fell silent.

She got rid of the garbage and leftovers from our dinner and sat at the foot of the bed, wearing one of my T-shirts. It was too big for her, but not by a great deal.

"Are you all right?" she asked.

"Yes."

"Would you like to cry now?"

I thought that over. "Yeah, I think I'd like to do that now."

She moved up next to me and took me in her arms and held me.

Later I said to her, "I hope I didn't take you away from anything."

"Well, I did have a date," she said.

"You did?"

She nodded.

"With who?"

"Philip."

"Who's Philip?"

"He works at the gallery, where I have my new job."

"What does he do?"

"Oh, he's my boss."

"Your boss?"

"Yes."

"Well . . . I hope you won't get in trouble for breaking the date with him."

"I don't think so," she said, smiling. "I told him I had to sit with a sick friend."

$\triangledown$

23

I WOKE THE NEXT morning to the smell of bacon and with only a slight headache. I didn't remember having any bacon in the place. I got up and padded naked to the closet to get my robe. She must have heard the closet door open.

"Take a shower and breakfast will be ready," she shouted from the kitchen.

"I didn't know I had any bacon," I shouted back.

"You didn't," she said. "I went out and got it."

"Very enterprising."

I took a shower and when I came into the kitchen wearing my robe, breakfast was on the table. Bacon, scrambled eggs, and toast.

"I would have made home fries," she said, putting a cup of coffee in front of me, "but you didn't have any potatoes around."

"You went out for the bacon," I said.

"I'm not your wife," she said, sitting opposite me. "I'm not going to do your shopping for you."

She may not have been my wife, but after we finished she did the dishes and cleaned up, then went to take her own shower.

"I have to go to work," she said, reappearing in the kitchen a few minutes later.

"I know."

"Will you be all right?"

"I'm fine," I said. "I just needed . . . a friend."

She came over to the table and took my hand.

"You've got one."

I kissed her hand and she left.

"Mr. Novak?"

"Arthur Novak, yes. Who is this?"

"My name is Miles Jacoby, Mr. Novak," I said. "I'm . . . I was a friend of Packy Moran's."

"Oh, yes," he said. "I read about it in this morning's newspaper. Terrible thing."

"Yes, it is. Listen, I wanted to let you know that I picked up Packy's things from the police."

"His things?"

"Personal effects—keys, wallet, watch, that sort of thing."

"Oh, I see."

"I also went to his place and took out his books, which I'll turn over to his accountant."

"Yes . . . well, that's very helpful of you, Mr. Jacoby. Do you have the man's address?"

"Name and address, yes."

"Since Mr. Moran had no family that I can recall, will you be handling the arrangements?"

"Yes, I will."

"Very well," he said. "I'll be in touch with you about the will."

"The will?"

"Yes, Mr. Moran left a will. I will read it after he has been buried. Perhaps he . . . left you something."

"Packy?" I said. "What would he have had to leave me? I'd rather have him alive."

"Yes, well, so would we all, Mr. Jacoby. Could you leave me your address and phone number, please, so that I may get in touch with you?"

I gave it to him and hung up.

I had called Heck as soon as Alison left. He had answered the phone himself, which was just as well. I wasn't really in the mood to talk to Missy.

Heck commiserated with me about Packy, whom he had never met. I asked him if he knew Novak, and in the nicest possible way he told me the man was an asshole.

He was right.

"Oh, Miles . . . "

"Yeah, Heck?"

"I talked to Mr. Scalesi."

"Oh, yeah?"

"He said that he is willing to talk to you."

"Okay, Heck," I said. "Maybe later, this week, huh? I'll call you."

There was a pause, and then he said, "All right, Miles. Again, I am sorry about your friend."

"Thanks, Heck."

I hung up. I knew why he had paused. He was wondering whether I was going to forget everything else now that Packy had been killed. Maybe he was wondering whether I was going to go after the Backshooter.

I wondered about it, too, for a while, but in the end I gave in to reality. The only thing that was going to catch the Backshooter was dumb luck, and it would be the cops who would catch him, just like with the Son of Sam.

An independent operator like me wouldn't stand a chance of catching a random serial killer.

As for forgetting everything else, that thought had entered my mind, too. So far, I didn't know what to do with it.

24

"THAT'S A LONG TIME to spend on one beer," Billy Palmer said, taking the stool next to me.

"Sorry," I said. "Is there a minimum per hour?"

"Not at all," he said. "In fact, I'm glad to see it."

"Good."

"I'm sorry about Packy."

"Yeah, thanks,"

"I guess you want to be alone, huh?"

"If you don't mind, Billy," I said, trying not to sound like I was brushing him off.

"I don't mind, Jack," he said, slapping me on the back. "Have something to eat, okay? On me."

"Sure."

I had gone to see Packy's accountant and had turned Packy's books and ledgers over to him. He told me how sorry he was that Packy was dead, and thanked me for bringing the stuff. From there I'd gone to Bogie's, where I'd been sitting with the same beer for half an hour—as much as I wanted to drink it down and order another.

By the time I got to the bottom of the bottle, the beer was warm and I was longing for a cold one. I knew if I gave in, though, and had a second I'd go ahead and have a third and fourth . . .

"How much for the beer, Stuart?" I asked.

"It's on me, Jack."

"Thanks," I said, not bothering to argue. I gave him more than the beer was worth as a tip and left.

I borrowed some gloves from Willy Wells and worked the heavy bag for a while. I was panting by the time I quit, but the craving for a cold beer was gone. Now I would have settled for some cold water!

Willy had been surprised when I showed up at the Forty-second Street Gym.

"Decided to try that comeback?" he had asked.

"I just need a workout," I said. "Do you have some gloves I can use?"

"Sure," he said. "No problem. Go ahead and change."

I'd stopped at my place for some sweats and shoes, but I hadn't brought my old gloves. Willy had given me a locker and I accepted the borrowed gloves from him and changed.

"Do you want to spar?" he had asked after I'd changed.

"And get killed?" I said. "No thanks. The heavy bag will do, for now."

Now that I was finished my hands were hanging at my side as if they weighed a ton each. Willy came up alongside me and stared.

"What?" I asked.

"You're in terrible shape."

"I know."

"Come back every day, kid," he said. "We'll get you back in shape."

"Might not be such a bad idea," I said, panting, pulling off the gloves. "If I don't have a heart attack first."

The M.E. released Packy's body two days later and I buried him in Holy Cross Cemetery in Brooklyn, near where his parents were buried. I hadn't announced it, and I was the only one in attendance. Packy wouldn't have wanted a big fuss.

Over the course of those two days and the two immediately following, I managed to work off the craving for a drink at the gym. I also began to run early in the morning. I'd already lost five pounds, and was starting to get my wind back. I'd stopped drinking beer altogether.

I'd also stopped talking to people. I didn't answer my phone or the door buzzer. On the morning of the fifth day I'd just come out of the shower after my morning run when the phone rang.

I answered.

"Miles?"

It was Caroline McWilliams.

"My God," she said, "I've been worried sick. Where have you been? I've been calling and calling. I went to Bogie's but they said they hadn't seen you in days, and—"

"Caroline," I said, cutting her off.

I told her about Packy, and she was sympathetic for about five minutes.

"I'm sorry you lost your friend, Miles," she said, "but what about Andy?"

"Caroline," I said, "Andy was killed by the Backshooter. It's about time you accepted that."

"No!" she said. "I don't believe it!"

"Caroline—"

"If you won't help me anymore, I'll just keep looking on my own!"

"Car—"

"I thought I could trust you, Miles," she said. "I thought . . ."

She hung up, and I did likewise. I felt badly for her, but it really was time she got on with her life, and maybe it was time I got on with mine. Maybe it *was* time for a comeback.

$\triangledown$

25

A LOT HAPPENED OVER the next few days.

Perhaps the most startling development to me was the news that Packy had left me his bar. Somehow that possibility had never occurred to me. I had no idea what I was going to do with it, and talked to Billy Palmer about it.

"I don't know if I can say anything that will help you, Jack," Billy said at one point. "I *can* tell you one thing, though."

"What's that?"

"Anybody who would want to be in this business has to be crazy."

Well, if I did choose to keep Packy's open, it wouldn't operate on the level that Bogie's did. Billy Palmer's place was a restaurant with a bar, while Packy's place had always been a saloon that served *some* food. I talked to an ex-cop P.I. named Sal Carlucci who ran a saloon in Greenpoint, Brooklyn, that was more on the order of Packy's. He said that if I did decide to keep the place open he hoped I would do better business than he did with his place.

On top of all that was happening I received two phone calls at Bogie's that intrigued me. One was from a man named Jules Van Voorhies. The name rang a bell, and then I remembered that I'd heard it from Walker Blue. He was the client referred by Caroline McWilliams who had an office in the Trump Tower. He was also a man Walker Blue said he didn't like. Van Voorhies apparently wanted to see me badly enough to call Bogie's looking for me.

There was another message that intrigued me, and that was from Heck Delgado's client *Don Salvatore Scalesi*! Don Salvatore also wanted to see me—not in a Trump Tower office, but in the Tombs, where he was presently being held on a murder charge without bail. Calls from such powerful, wealthy men were hard to ignore.

The other thing that intrigued me—or *bothered* me, really—was that there were no messages from Caroline McWilliams. Guilt played a big part in my concern. I kept remembering what she had said to me the last time we spoke, before she hung up on me. The word "trust" kept echoing in my head.

I was sitting in Bogie's drinking coffee-my drink of preference of late—and holding the message from Van Voorhies in one hand and the one from Scalesi in the other hand when Billy came up behind me.

"Stuart's very impressed," he said.

I looked around, figuring that for Stuart to be impressed some pretty young thing must have just walked into the place.

Not seeing anyone that qualified I asked, "Impressed with what?"

"With you."

"Me?" I stared at Billy as if he were crazy. "What the hell for?"

"Those messages you're holding," Billy said. "Those are some high powered names."

"I can see how he'd recognize Scalesi's name," I said, looking down at the paper. "It's been on the front page enough times." I looked at Billy and asked, "But what does he know about Jules Van Voorhies?"

Billy shrugged and said, "I guess he plays the stock market."

"Come again?"

"Van Voorhies is a high-powered trader in the market," Billy said. "Stuart reads the financial section of the *New York Times*."

"What else do you know about him?"

"I don't know anything about him," Billy said. "I only know what Stuart said. Excuse me, I've got an order coming in."

After Billy left my side I waved Stuart over.

"More coffee?" Stuart asked.

"No. Tell me what you know about Jules Van Voorhies," I said.

"Well, he trades in the market in a big way," Stuart said, leaning on his elbows. "He owns a lot of companies and at least one sports team that I know of. He owns race horses *and* dogs, and I think he's planning to build a casino hotel in Atlantic City."

I was dumbfounded.

"How do you know all of that?"

Stuart pulled out a magazine from beneath the bar and showed it to me.

"I read *Forbes*."

"Is there anything in there about him?" I asked, starting to reach for the magazine.

"Not in this issue," he said, "but there was a piece on him a few months back."

"Would you still have that issue at home?"

"I don't know, but I'll check," he said, standing up straight as a new customer came in. "If I have it I'll bring it in tomorrow."

"I'd appreciate it, Stuart."

"Sure, Jack, are you—" he started, but he was interrupted when the phone rang. He waved at the new customer and went to answer it. He listened for a moment and then walked it over to me.

I took it and said, "Jacoby."

"You'd better get over to New York Hospital," Hocus said. He sounded tense.

"What for?"

"A friend of yours is there."

I wondered why he was being so cagey.

"Who?"

"Caroline McWilliams."

"What?" I stared at the phone the way people do when they're not sure they've heard something right.

"She's been beaten up pretty bad, Jack."

Jesus.

"What happened?"

"I'll tell you when you get here."

"I'll be right there." I started to put the phone down, then lifted it to my mouth again and asked, "Hocus, did she ask for me?"

"No," Hocus said, "she specifically asked that you *not* be contacted."

I left Bogie's fast, wearing my guilt on my sleeve for everyone to see.

26

NEW YORK HOSPITAL IS on York Avenue in the upper Seventies. It did not escape me that the location was close to Caroline's apartment. That made me think of two possible scenarios to explain what had happened. This was, after all, New York City, and Caroline just might have been mugged. Or she might have continued to look into her husband's death and somehow, somewhere, had stepped on somebody's toes.

When I reached the hospital Hocus was waiting for me in the lobby.

"How is she?" I asked.

"She's banged up."

"Serious?"

"She won't be leaving right away."

Why did I feel like I was having to drag answers out of him?

"This way," he said, and I followed.

"How did you get involved in this?" I asked. "Where was she attacked?"

"In the lobby of her apartment building."

"In the *lobby*," I said. "Did she get a look at the guy?"

"No," Hocus said. "The light in the lobby was out, and she couldn't see his face in the dark."

"Jesus, doesn't she know better than to walk into a dark lobby?" I said. "Was it a mugging?"

"Doubtful," Hocus said. "The guy made no attempt to try for her wallet, he just beat her up."

"He didn't say anything?"

"Not that she mentioned."

We stepped into an elevator and he pressed the button for the fifth floor.

"You didn't answer my question."

"Which question was that?"

"How did you get involved?" I repeated. "This is not your balliwick."

"They asked her who to notify," Hocus said, "and she gave them my name."

"Why you?"

"Apparently she's got no family."

"Yeah, but still, why you?"

"You mean, why not you?"

"Well . . . why not me?"

Hocus shrugged and said, "I guess you'll have to ask her that."

"I will."

The elevator stopped. We got off and he turned right, with me a step behind him. I followed him down the long corridor until we finally reached her room and entered.

She was lying on her back on the bed. I could see that her

left arm was in a cast, and there was a bandage on her right cheek. The right eye was almost swollen shut, but the left was bright and alert.

"Miles!"

"Hocus, can you leave us alone for a few minutes?" I asked.

"Uh, sure, I'll just, uh, wait outside."

I waited until he left to speak.

"Just what the hell are you trying to do?" I demanded.

"*I* didn't do anything," she said. "It was done *to* me, in case you haven't noticed."

I moved closer to the bed and said, "Tell me what happened."

She gave me basically the same the same story she'd given Hocus. She had arrived home and inserted her key into the lobby door. As she stepped inside she realized that it was dark. Before she could take another step someone grabbed her and started beating her.

"He just grabbed you?" I said. "He didn't say anything to you?"

"No," she said. "He didn't speak, and I didn't see his face. I got the impression he was a big man, though, when he started bouncing me off the walls."

"He didn't try for your wallet?"

"No."

"He didn't give you some kind of warning?"

"No," she said, and she bit her bottom lip, which had started to tremble. 'I . . . I thought he was going to kill me, Miles!"

Her right hand came up and I caught it in mine. She squeezed mine so tightly she cut off my circulation.

"Easy," I said. Finally, she loosened her grip and I flexed my fingers, keeping them intertwined with hers.

"Now, Caroline, suppose you tell me what you've been doing all week."

"I've been looking into those cases of Andy's. You know, the ones you were interested in."

"Did you go to see the people?"

"No. I did most of it by phone from the office in the apartment."

"But you did see some of them?"

She shrugged and said, "Two or three."

"Did anyone say anything to you that might be interpreted as a threat?"

"No," she said. She looked at me and said, "You think this has something to do with Andy's death?"

"I'm not a believer in coincidence, Caroline," I said. "He didn't go after your wallet, and I assume he didn't try to sexually—"

"No."

"Well, then you must have rattled somebody's chain, and this is a not so very subtle message."

"Jesus," she said. She tried to lift her left arm, hissed in pain, and then released my hand and put her right hand to her forehead.

"You'll be all right here for a while," I said. "How badly are you hurt?"

"Broken arm, broken rib. They x-rayed my cheekbone to see if it's fractured. They haven't gotten the results yet, though."

"Then you'll be here a few days."

"I suppose."

"I'll have someone come and sit with you."

"A policeman?"

"If I can, otherwise I'll just hire somebody I can trust."

"And what are you going to do?"

"I'll poke around a little, see what I can find out."

"Does this mean you're going to help me again, Miles?"

"Sure," I said, "yeah, Caroline, I'm going to help you again."

"Out of guilt?"

I hesitated, then nodded and said, "That's a big part of it."

"What's the little part of it?"

I leaned over and kissed her gently on the lips, noticing that the lower one was puffy.

"I'm sorry you got beaten up, Caroline."

"I'm not," she said. "It means somebody doesn't want Andy's death looked into. *That* means he wasn't killed by the Backshooter."

"That's your logic," I said, "and I'm inclined to agree. The cops, however, don't usually subscribe to that brand of logic."

"Talk to Hocus."

"Hocus is here as a favor," I said, "to me or to you, I don't know which. Tell me, why did you have the hospital call him and not me?"

She shrugged.

"You were out of it, and I know Hocus slightly because he knew Andy . . . slightly . . . "

I frowned, wondering if I had ever mentioned to her that I knew Hocus. Would she be above using her injury to draw me back into the case? And if she wasn't, could I blame her? She wanted to know who killed her husband, after all, and was entitled to.

I decided to accept her explanation.

"Who's the detective on the case?" I asked.

"His name is Leadman. He took my statement, and then I think he talked to Hocus."

"All right, I'll talk to Hocus, too."

She brought her hand down from her head and I took it.

"Miles—" she said.

It was as if I could read her mind. I knew she wanted to talk about—for want of a better word—us.

"We'll talk about that another time," I said, squeezing her hand.

She might have tried to pursue the matter if the nurse hadn't come in at that point.

"Time for your shot, Mrs. McWilliams."

"I'll try to get back later tonight," I said, "by tomorrow for sure."

"What about—"

"I won't leave here until I have someone to watch you," I promised.

"Miles—"

"Just be quiet and let the nice nurse jab you in your pretty butt."

The nurse glared at me, holding the syringe in her right hand menacingly. I left the room.

$\triangledown$

27

HOCUS AGREED TO HAVE a police officer sit at Caroline's door at least overnight, or until I could have someone relieve him.

"You know Leadman?" I asked on the way back down in the elevator.

"Yeah, we go back some. He's . . . competent."

"Bent?"

"To a certain degree."

"He won't hold you up on putting a uniform on her door?"

"No, but he won't like it. He thinks it was a mugging or a rape gone bad. He figures she resisted and the guy went crazy and beat her up, then forgot what he came for and took off."

"Any witnesses?"

"No, none."

"What do you think?"

He shrugged. "What do you think?"

"I think she asked the wrong questions about her husband around the wrong guy."

"There was no threat."

"The beating is an implied threat."

"We can't deal in implied threats."

"I know that," I said. "That's why I'm going to have someone watch her for a while."

"While you do what?"

"While I ask around."

"Where?"

"The same places she did," I said. "Maybe the same goon will come after me."

"And kill you."

"I'm not a woman."

"And he won't treat you like one," Hocus said. "If he comes after you he'll do it with one thing in mind."

"Then you agree with me?"

"I didn't say that."

"I know," I said. "I noticed you were very careful not to."

In the lobby Hocus said, "I have my car. Give you a ride?"

"As far downtown as you're going," I said. "I can get the rest of the way on my own."

"Want to stop someplace for a drink?"

"What is this," I asked, "a test? No, I do not want a drink."

"What are you going to do, then?"

"I have to make arrangements for Caroline to be watched," I said, and then while fingering the two pieces of paper in my pocket I added, "and then I have a couple of messages to answer."

28

RAY CARBONE AND I once had a lot in common. Although he was only three years older than me, both Ray and I had been "retired" from the ring during our last fight. An un-ranked middleweight throughout his career, Ray was prob-ably the most respected unranked middleweight of his time. He was the guy managers put their fighters in with when they wanted their boys to have a *tough* fight. I had used him a time or two in the past for some bodyguard work, and I'd heard that he'd gone into it full time now.

When I got back to my apartment I called his number and found him in.

"How's it hangin', Jack?" he said. "What can I do for ya?"

"I need you to do some bodyguard work, Ray," I said. "Are you free?"

"For how long?"

"I'm not sure," I said. I told him about Caroline—who she was and what had happened to her.

"Hey, sure, Jack," he said. "I hadn't forgotten that you got me started in this business. You want me to start tonight?"

"I'd appreciate it, Ray."

"You got it, buddy."

"What's your fee—"

"You pay what I'm worth, Jack," Ray said. "I trust ya. Ex-pugs got to stick together, you know?"

I thought of Packy, another ex-pug and said, "We sure do, Ray. Thanks again. There's a cop on her door now, but I'll call ahead and let him know you're coming."

I hung up and called Hocus, who said he'd call the hospital and tell the cop to expect Carbone.

That done, I pulled out two messages I'd gotten at Bogie's. There was a phone number on Van Voorhie's message, but not on Scalesi's. The latter was easily solved by calling Heck Delgado.

"Hi, Missy, is Heck in?"

"Hi, Jack. How are you?"

Her question was asked with some hesitancy, and I realized that I hadn't spoken to her or Heck in over a week. Since I considered Missy to be one of my best friends in the world, I felt ashamed.

"I'm fine, Missy," I said.

"Really?"

"Yes, really. Is the boss there?"

"Hold on."

She was gone for about ten seconds, and when she came back on she said, "He'll be right with you Jack. Uh, come and see me sometime?"

"You can count on it, beautiful."

"You know something? You *sound* better."

"I am," I said. "I swear."

"Here's Heck."

"Jack, how the hell are you?"

"I'm fine, Heck."

"Getting back into it?"

"In a big way," I said. "I got a message from Scalesi. Can you get me in to see him?"

"They already have your name, Jack. Just identify yourself and you're in."

"How's your case going?"

"Not good. With Two-John gone I don't really have a hole card."

"I'll see if I can turn one up for you."

"I'm glad you're back, my friend," Heck said.

"Yeah, me too. See ya."

I hung up, then picked up the receiver and dialed the number for Jules Van Voorhies.

"Who may I say is calling?" a woman's voice asked.

"Miles Jacoby."

"And what is it in reference to?"

"I'm returning his call."

"One moment."

It was more like five minutes, but finally she came back on.

"Mr. Jacoby? I'm sorry, but Mr. Van Voorhies cannot come to the phone at the moment. He has instructed me to ask you to come to his office tomorrow at eleven A.M. Would that be possible?"

"Tell him I'll be there," I said. "Thank you."

"Of course, sir," she said, and hung up.

I checked my watch. It was seven o'clock, too late to go down to the Tombs. I decided to stop by there early tomor-

row morning to see Scalesi, and then go uptown to see Van
Voorhies. Where would that leave me?

2 9

I THINK THE WAY I felt sitting across from Don Salvatore
Scalesi is the way Stephen King wants people to feel when
they read one of his books.

Not that he was a scary *looking* man. It was more what I
knew he represented. Actually, he was slick looking, like a
maitre d' in a classy restaurant. Even though he was wearing
prison clothes, he still had his pinky rings, and his cologne,
and his black hair was slicked down, lending to the sleek
look. He was in his sixties, and his hair and eyebrows
unnaturally black, the color of black shoe polish.

On my arrival, I had mentioned his name, Heck Delgado's
name, and then my own. It was an ego lift that *my* name
seemed to carry the most weight. They made me feel that if
I had been anyone else, I wouldn't have gotten in to see
Scalesi.

Now that I was sitting across from New York's number

one crime boss," as the papers called him, I didn't quite know what to say. (Actually, whichever "crime boss," happens to be on trial at the moment is usually called New York's number one crime boss by the papers).

"You're Jacoby?" he asked.

I nodded.

On the table in front of us was a gold cigarette case, a heavy, marble ashtray, and a cup of coffee. Actually, it looked like *expresso*. He had a cigarette in one hand and was fiddling with a gold lighter with the other.

"You used to fight."

"For a while."

"Why'd you quit?"

"I got knocked out."

"You should have gotten up again," Scalesi said. "When you get knocked down, you get up. If you don't . . . " he said, shrugging.

"I got knocked down once too often and decided to call it quits."

He shrugged again, this time using only his facial muscles—a very Italian gesture—and said, "That's a smart move, too. Get out before you get hurt."

"I thought so."

"I hear you're working for me."

"I'm working for Heck Delgado."

"Yeah," Scalesi said, "my lawyer. You're working for him, you're working for me."

"It doesn't quite work that way."

"Why not?"

This wasn't what I had come here to talk about.

"You pay Heck, but you don't pay me."

"That means I can't fire you?"

This time I shrugged.

"If you think I can't—"

"Mr. Scalesi," I said, interrupting him. I wanted to try to make a point. "If you want to impress me, I'm impressed already—with your reputation. If you want to scare me, you're going to have to try a lot harder than this."

"Aye," he said, smiling. "A tough guy."

"If you want to talk," I said, "let's talk."

I sat back, waiting to see how he was going to react.

"All right," he said, after a moment. "I understand my only witness is dead."

"Jenny Wheeler," I said. "Yeah, she's dead."

"Well, you see. I think that should be enough for the cops to cut me loose, but they don't figure it that way."

"How do *you* figure it that way?" I asked.

"Simple," he said with a shrug. "She could've cleared me, and somebody killed her to keep her from doing that."

"And what if you sent some of your . . . associates to kill her so the police would think that way?"

He narrowed his eyes at me and sat forward.

"You're a smart kid, Jacoby."

He pronounced *Ja-co-bee*. I corrected him.

"It's Jack-uh-bee."

"Yeah, Miles, right?"

"Right."

"Look, Miles," he said. "I need a smart P.I. on my case. You were smart enough to know when to quit fighting, and you're smart enough to know when to talk back to me, I want to hire you."

"I'm already working for Heck Delgado."

"Yeah, but I want you working for me," Scalesi said. "I'll pay you double what my spic lawyer's payin' you."

"Sorry," I said. "I'll work on your case, but I work for Delgado—and he's not a spic. He's a wetback."

"A what?"

"Mexican-American," I said. "A chicano."

"Okay, whatever you say," Scalesi said, leaning back. "I don't mean any offense."

"I'm sure you don't, and neither do I. I'll continue to work for Delgado."

"Work for who you want," Scalesi said, "just find out who killed that whore. It's my last chance to prove I didn't do my wife."

"Who did?"

"What?"

"If you didn't kill her, who did?"

Apparently he wasn't prepared for that question. I was sure he must have been asked it before, by Delgado if by no one else.

"I don't know."

"No ideas?"

"No."

"Were you and she having—"

"Aye!" he said. "I didn't send for you to ask me a bunch of questions!"

"If you want me to help you I'll need to know everything."

"Read the file," he said. "Haven't you read it already?"

"No, Heck hasn't shown it to me."

"Well why the fuck not?"

"Because all he hired me to do was find Two-John Wheeler."

"And now?"

"And now I want to find out who killed her. If you didn't kill your wife, maybe the same person who did also killed Two-John."

He stared at me for a moment, and then smiled. He took a cigarette from his case and lit it with the gold lighter.

"I knew you were smart. All right, I'll tell the—I'll tell Delgado to show you the whole file."

"How about answering my—"

"I've answered all the damned questions I'm going to!" he snapped. "Read the file."

"All right," I said, getting up.

I started for the door, then stopped and turned back.

"What?" he asked.

"Did you know Two-John Wheeler?"

"I said read—"

"I'm sure the real answer to that is not in the file," I said.

He stared at me, then said, "I knew her."

"How good a witness would she have been for you?"

"The best."

"Why do you say that?"

He smiled and said, "Because she had my dick in her mouth at the time I was supposed to be killing my wife."

30

MY NEXT STOP WAS the Trump Tower. Jules Van Voorhies had his name on the directory, which came in handy since his secretary hadn't told me what floor his office was one.

It was on twenty-nine.

When I got off the elevator there was no need for me to look for his office. It was obvious that he had the entire floor. Three steps out of the elevator and I was facing a reception desk. On the wall behind it, in large gold letters, it said VAN VOORHIES, LTD. From what I knew about the man—which wasn't much, admittedly—he didn't seem to have any limits.

"Yes?" the receptionist said. She had not come by the job right out of secretarial school it seemed. She was in her late thirties and perfectly made up to hide any blemishes she might have had. She had done a fine job. Her face looked perfect, like that of a department store mannequin. Her eyes had all the warmth of one, too.

"Miles Jacoby," I said.

She stared at me.

"I have an appointment with Mr. Van Voorhies."

Suddenly an artificial smile appeared, but there was still no warmth in the eyes.

"Yes, sir. Wait just a moment, please." She picked up the phone and dialed three numbers, and told someone that I was there to see Mr. Van Voorhies. She hung up and gave me the smile again, "Mr. Van Voorhies's private secretary will be right with you."

"Is she the only one who knows where his office is?" I asked.

She looked at me without comprehension, and I decided to skip it.

I had no sooner sat down and picked up a copy of *Time* magazine then a woman's voice said, "Mr. Jacoby?"

"Yes."

I stood up and faced her. She was fortyish, handsome, and well cared for. She was not as perfect as the receptionist—for one thing there was a lipstick smear on one of her front teeth—but at least there was genuine warmth in her eyes as she smiled at me. I found that odd because she'd been anything but friendly yesterday on the telephone.

"Please follow me."

I did. On the way she asked if I would like coffee. I said I would. We reached an unmarked door and she knocked on it and opened it without waiting for a reply.

"Mr. Jacoby, sir." She stood aside and said, "Please go in. I'll bring your coffee shortly."

"Thank you."

I entered the office and she closed the door behind me.

Van Voorhies was sitting behind the largest desk I'd ever seen, in front of a huge window that undoubtedly looked out over Fifth Avenue.

"Please, Mr. Jacoby, take a seat."

He pronounced my name correctly.

Van Voorhies stood up. He was in his late forties, or a very well-kept early fifties, and he was tall and slender. His hair was dark, but unlike Scalesi's it was naturally so. He was clean shaven and his cologne was subtle. I hadn't yet detected an accent, but he hadn't said much.

I came forward and he extended his hand. I shook it briefly before sitting. His grip was firm, but very curt. He had large hands.

"This is awkward," he said.

"Take your time."

He gave me a fleeting, humorless smile, looked at his watch, and said, "Um, yes."

The secretary entered and set three cups of coffee on the desk.

"Thank you," I said.

She left without acknowledging me.

I picked up the cup closest to me and sipped it while I waited for him to speak. He looked at his watch again. Finally, I got impatient—or maybe I just wanted to show off.

"Who are we waiting for?"

"I beg your pardon?"

I nodded toward his desk and said, "The third cup of coffee, and you keep looking at your watch. Who are we waiting for?"

"Um, yes, very good," he said. "We are waiting for my attorney."

"I see," I said. "Is there something we're going to discuss that requires—"

"I'm sorry I'm late, Jules," a man said, bursting into the office. "Is this him?"

He was a tall, well-built man in his thirties. He had the kind of face that probably would have brought warmth even to the receptionist's eyes—a strong cleft chin and Paul Newman blue eyes. Some day they'll make crayons and name the colors after movie stars—Paul Newman blue, Elizabeth Taylor violet, and on like that. He had Paul's eyes.

"I'm him," I said. "Who are you?"

"Calvin Natt," he said, extending his hand. He shook mine exactly once and dropped it. "How much as Jules told you?"

"Nothing," I said, reseating myself. "Your coffee is here."

"What? Oh, thanks." He moved to the desk, picked up the coffee, and took a healthy swig.

"All right, Jules," he said. That was Van Voorhies's cue to proceed, I guess, because that's what he did.

"Some time back I hired Andy McWilliams to do a job for me. He subcontracted the job out to Walker Blue. I was happy with that. I know Blue by reputation."

"Then why did you hire Andy?"

"He was recommended to me."

"By whom?"

"By me," Natt said. "I'd used him before on some minor things."

"Minor," I said. I looked at Van Voorhies and said, "Go on."

"We had two meetings with Walker Blue, during which we discussed what we wanted to do."

"We meaning you and Mr. Natt here?"

"Yes."

Natt sipped his coffee again, but his eyes peered over the cup at me. I had the feeling he was sizing me up for something.

"What did you hire him to do?"

Van Voorhies stared at me a moment.

"He didn't tell you?"

"He did not."

He exchanged a satisfied glance with Natt, who nodded sagely. I had the feeling he was saying, "I told you so."

"How much do you know about me, Mr. Jacoby?"

"Not much," I said. "I know you're wealthy and that you own a lot of toys."

"Uh, yes," he said. "I suppose it would seem that way to some people."

"To some," I agreed. I set the coffee cup back down on his desk. It was lousy coffee.

"I have political ambitions."

"Surprise, surprise," I said. "I'd be surprised if you didn't."

"I wanted Walker Blue to . . . look into my past."

"Jules—" Natt said, and now I had the impression that Van Voorhies had said more than his lawyer thought advisable.

"Looking for what?" I asked. "Skeletons?" This sounded weird to me.

"Mr. Jacoby—" Natt said, but I didn't give him a chance to deposit his two cents.

"You hired Walker Blue—through Andy McWilliams—to check yourself out?"

Van Voorhies looked up at Natt as if to ask "What should I say?"

It was too late for that.

"It was merely a precaution," Calvin Natt said.

"Against what?"

"Accidents."

I looked away from Natt to Van Voorhies.

"Mr. Van Voorhies, we're playing word games here. *Do* you or do you *not* have skeletons in your closet?"

Van Voorhies opened his mouth to answer but Natt jumped in. "Don't answer that," he said.

I stared at him a few moments. "All right, let's do it the easy way. Why did you want me to come up here?"

"We were just wondering what you might have found out," Natt said.

"About what?"

"About . . . Mr. Van Voorhies."

I ignored Natt.

"Mr. Van Voorhies, have you spoken to Andy McWilliams's widow lately."

"Yes," he said. "She called and I asked her to come up."

"To ask her the same question you just asked me?"

They both hesitated and then Van Voorhies said, "Yes."

"What did she say?"

"She said she was not interested in my past, only in who killed her husband."

"And of course you know nothing about her husband's death."

"No, I do not," he said. "How did he die?"

"He was apparently killed by the Backshooter,' Calvin Natt said.

"'Apparently' being the key word," I said.

"You don't think he was?" Natt asked.

"I'm keeping an open mind."

"That's what we were hoping for on your part—" Natt said, "an open mind."

"Are you willing to pay me for what I know?" I asked.

"Of course," Natt said, "but you will have to sign a contract."

"A contract?"

"Of employment," Natt said. "You would be working for me—at a very generous fee, of course."

"Of course."

I thought about that for a moment, then realized why I'd be working for Natt instead of directly for Van Voorhies. In working for a lawyer, I'd be bound by his right of client confidentiality.

"Did Andy sign this contract?"

"He did."

"And Walker Blue?"

"Yes."

I studied both of them for a moment while *they* studied me, hopeful expressions on their faces. They were afraid that I already knew something, and were now trying to buy not only my silence, but me.

And I didn't know a damned thing.

"Mr. Van Voorhies, I have no desire whatsoever to look into your past, unless Andy McWilliams's murder is part of it."

"That's absurd."

"It probably is," I said. I stood up and prepared to leave.

"Wait a moment," Natt said. "Would you be willing to turn over any, er, pertinent information to us—if you discover anything relating to Mr. Van Voorhies?"

If I said no, would I be the next one they'd try to beat up? It might be worth finding out.

I did what Caroline had probably done. I turned and left without answering them. She probably hadn't liked them anymore than I did.

$\triangledown$

3 1

On my way uptown on the subway I thought over my morning interviews and came to the same conclusion about both "powerful" men. They were scared!

Scalesi was facing a murder rap, and if what he said about Two-John Wheeler was true—that she was with him at the time his wife was supposed to have been killed—then his best chance of acquittal had gone down the tubes with her murder. He could have been scared because after all the crimes he had committed, he was going to bite the big one for something he didn't do. Also, it made sense to me that someone might have killed her to make sure he took the fall.

If he was innocent.

He could have been getting an A-1 blow-job from Two-John and still *had* his wife killed by someone else. He might have been scared because he was guilty and knew he was going to be found so. Scalesi's behavior made sense to me at either angle.

Van Voorhies, on the other hand, made my head spin. Here was a man with political ambitions who must have had something so hot in his closet that he had to hire a P.I. to try to find it, just to see if he had hidden it well enough. His angle was that the P.I.—Andy, or whoever—would be working for his lawyer, and would therefore be bound by the lawyer's client confidentiality. But client confidentiality is such a technical point. It's like the Catholic priest's seal of the confessional. The silence is professional, which means that the man—a priest, a lawyer, a doctor—can still talk, if he is willing to give up his career. If Andy had talked he would have damaged his credibility as far as other lawyers hiring him, but what if he felt that what he had to say was worth that? Was that why he was killed? To keep silent? Then again, he hadn't worked on the case, Walker Blue had, and no one tried to kill Walker Blue. If Walker *had* found out something, he had kept it to himself, ensuring his own safety.

Caroline had probably walked out on Van Voorhies and his lawyer, which had gotten her beaten up. They probably felt she knew nothing, and wanted to keep it that way.

But what about me? What did they think I knew? Maybe I'd made a mistake walking out on them, but I didn't like them because had felt they could buy me. I'm a single guy with little in the way of responsibilities, so I could afford to sneer at Van Voorhies's money. If I'd been married with three kids, a dog, a car payment, and two mortgages, I would probably have jumped at the offer—even though I didn't know anything.

I wondered what Van Voorhies had to hide. Was he afraid that some nude photos of his with a girl—or a guy or a *dog*—were going to queer his chance to be mayor or governor or whatever?

It was possible, of course, that he knew nothing at all about Andy McWilliams's death. There were still some of Andy's other clients to talk to but first I wanted to stop in and see how Caroline and Ray were getting along.

$\bigtriangledown$

3 2

Ray CARBONE WAS SITTING in a green plastic chair in front of the door to Caroline's room. He had put on some weight since I'd seen him last and was punishing the plastic pretty good, but he still looked like somebody you wouldn't want to tangle with. He'd taken more punches than I had in the ring and it showed on his face, especially on his nose and around the eyes. A couple of nurses walked past him and he exchanged glances with them before he saw me.

He stood up as I reached him.

"Hey, Jack," he said, sticking out his hand. "You look like you're in shape."

"Still a few pounds from fighting weight, Ray," I said, shaking his hand. "You've beefed up some. Making a comeback as a heavyweight?"

"I've put on a few."

I looked at the plastic chair.

"Couldn't you find something a little more comfortable to sit in?"

"Are you kidding?" he said. "I had to steal this from the cafeteria. I don't *want* to be comfortable. I might fall asleep, like the cop I relieved."

It was a good point.

"Why don't you get a cup of coffee?" I said. "I'll be here about twenty minutes or so."

"Okay," he said. "Oh, one thing we didn't discuss."

"What's that?"

"Is this a twenty-four hour job?"

It hit me then that I hadn't even thought about that.

"I mean, I don't mind," Ray continued, "but if it is, I'll need somebody to feed my cat."

"You have a cat?"

He nodded. "A Persian."

"I'll see if I can't get someone to relieve you tonight."

"If you get another man," Ray said, "I'll take the night shift."

"Okay."

He went off to get his coffee and I went into Caroline's room.

"Are you awake?"

"Miles?"

She turned her head on her pillow and looked at me. Her face looked more bruised than when I'd seen her last.

"Ooh," I said, moving to the bed, "technicolor."

"Oh," she said, raising her good hand to cover her face. "I must look awful."

"How do you feel?"

"Like I look."

I took her hand and held it.

"Did you meet Ray?"

"He introduced himself," she said. "Is he another ex-fighter?"

"He is. He fought as a middleweight, like I did."

"Really? Did you ever fight each other?"

"Once."

"Who won?"

"I'll never tell."

"Maybe I can get him to tell."

"I doubt it, but you're welcome to try. Look, Caroline, we have to talk about a few things."

"Okay," she said, "but I've had some painkillers, so if I ask you to repeat something, please understand."

"Okay."

I told her about my meeting with Jules Van Voorhies and she listened intently until I was finished.

"I didn't like him," she said. "He thought he could buy me."

"He probably believes he can buy anyone and anything."

"Well, if he's got something in his past that would keep him out of office," she said, with feeling, "I'd sure like to know about it."

I frowned as a thought occurred to me.

"Caroline, Andy's files on the cases from the P.I.'s he subcontracted work to were pretty skimpy. Did you look at them?"

"Of course."

"Did you see the file on Van Voorhies?"

She put her hand to her mouth.

"What is it?"

"I never had a chance to tell you. I thought it was funny none of the details of that case were given. I mean, there was a file, but all it had was a couple of names. I thought it was odd, because Andy was so good with files. Someone . . . "

she hesitated, then went on, "someone could have . . . taken the contents—My God!" she said.

"What?"

"The office was broken into."

"When?"

"Oh God," she said, putting her hand to her forehead, "it was the day of the funeral. I just thought it was those people who check obituaries and then break into people's homes."

"Was Andy's office address in the obit?"

"Oh God, I don't remember—I never noticed anything missing—Oh, why am I so dumb—"

"Don't get down on yourself," I said. "You're not dumb. There were a lot of files for you to go through. This means I'm going to *have* to get a look at Walker Blue's copy."

"Do you think that Van Voorhies had me beaten up?"

"The thought *had* occurred to me. Men like him generally try to buy you off first, and when that doesn't work—"

"That sonofabitch!"

"Now, take it easy," I said. "We don't know for sure that it was him."

"He's a sonofabitch, anyway."

"Right. No argument, there."

"What do you think he's afraid of?"

"Well, it's usually sex," I said, "but maybe he's a thief."

"If he was a thief," she said, "that wouldn't necessarily keep him out of public office."

"Touché. Caroline?"

"Yes?"

"Did Andy ever say anything to you about Van Voorhies? Like why he wouldn't work on the case himself?"

"No," she said, "nothing beyond the fact that he was subbing the job to Walker Blue."

"Why did he do that?"

"I didn't know at the time," she said, "but with everything we've discovered, I think I've got it figured out. You see, Andy *hated* politics, and did his best to avoid cases that had anything to do with it."

"Why take the Van Voorhies case at all then?"

"Money, I guess," she said. "He may not have liked politics, but he loved money."

I thought about him with that blonde on his arm and figured that if she wasn't the only one, then he probably had a need for a lot of money.

"Maybe he needed it too much," she added.

"We all need it."

"No," she said. "Andy was different. He liked to live higher than his means. He . . . had a lot of friends."

I stared at her, wondering if she was talking about friends, or *friends*.

"Maybe you should talk to Walker Blue," she said, through a yawn. "Oh, I'm sorry. Those painkillers put me to sleep."

"I'll leave you alone in a few minutes."

"No, no," she said sleepily, her eyes heavy-lidded. "I'm glad you're here."

"Caroline," I said uneasily, "I don't think I've apologized yet for . . . deserting you. I had a lot on my mind, although that's not much of an excuse, but I've gotten myself straightened out and I want you to know that I'll be here for you as long as you need me."

I looked at her and saw that her eyes were closed and she was breathing deeply and evenly. She had fallen asleep during my apology. I hoped she had heard some of it, because I didn't think I'd have the nerve to say it again.

I had wanted to ask her for the keys to her apartment but I didn't want to wake her. I went through the drawers of the flimsy night table until I found her keys and pocketed them. I didn't think she'd mind.

Outside, Ray had returned with two containers of coffee. He was working on one, and the other was underneath the chair.

"You know," he said, "I haven't seen a decent looking nurse in this place yet."

"Keep a sharp eye out," I said. "There's got to be one."

"Look, Jack," he said, twisting around in his chair. "I can do this job alone. I don't sleep much anymore anyway. Like I said, I just have to get someone to feed my cat."

"Let me have the keys to your place, Ray," I said, "and I'll feed the cat."

"Hey, thanks," he said, handing over the key. "The food's in the closet above the sink. Don't give him the same flavor twice in a row, though."

"Picky cat, huh?"

"Well, he is a Persian," Ray said, "not an alley cat."

"I'll keep that in mind."

33

I SPENT THE REST of the day talking to the clients Andy had had when he died, and the ones Po and Delvecchio had worked for. Some of them didn't like being questioned again, and when I told them it was in reference to Andy McWilliams's death some of them *really* got uptight.

By the time I finished I was just about convinced that none of them had anything to do with Andy McWilliams's death.

When I got back to my apartment I put a call in to Walker Blue's office, but his secretary told me he wasn't in. I left a message for him to call me. I wanted to know what he found out about Jules Van Voorhies.

I called Bogie's to ask Stuart if he had that copy of *Forbes*.

"I've got it right here behind the bar, Jack."

"I'll be over later to pick it up, Stuart. Thanks."

I wondered about Van Voorhies's political ambitions.

Maybe the Forbes article would give me his background. If
not, I'd have to make a trip to the main library on Forty-second Street. I wondered idly if "Van Voorhies" was even his
real name. Maybe that was what he was trying to hide.

Since I couldn't get Walker Blue on the phone I decided
to go to Bogie's and get that magazine. Maybe while I was
there I'd also have something to eat.

When I entered Bogie's, Stuart saw me right away and put
the magazine on the bar. As I climbed onto a stool I heard
some commotion in the dining room and took a look. The
round table in the corner was filled with people.

I ordered a Diet Coke and asked, "What's going on over
there?"

"Oh, a regular customer is having a little party," Stuart
said. "An editor named Seldman just got a new job. They're
celebrating."

"Editor?" I asked. "What does he edit?"

"What else?" Stuart said. "Mysteries."

I worked on my Coke and read the *Forbes* article. It told
me that Van Voorhies was actually born in this country to
Dutch parents who then took him to Europe to live. He came
back here and attended college at Harvard. As well as being
a big shot trader and sports and hotel mogul, he was a lawyer.
He wasn't yet in Donald Trump's class, but I guess that's
why *he* was renting in the *Trump Tower*, and not the other
way around.

"Another Coke?"

"And something to eat," I said. "I'll have some tortellini."

"A vegetable?"

"Some broccoli."

"Isn't that fattening?"

"Broccoli?"

"Tortellini."

"I'll work it off."

He shrugged and put the order through.

I was wading through the tortellini when the phone rang. Somehow I knew it was going to be for me and was ready when Stuart handed me the phone.

"Jacoby?" Hocus said.

"Is this more good news?" I asked.

"More of the same, buddy," he said. "They found your snitch."

"Binky?"

"Yep."

"Where?"

"In a cardboard box on Tenth Avenue," Hocus said.

"Dead?"

"Very."

"How?"

"The same as Two-John Wheeler, Jack," Hocus said. "His throat was cut."

I dropped my fork on my plate.

"Any reason for me to come down?"

"Not unless you like looking at bodies."

"How long was he there?"

"I'll know more when Doc Mahbee does the autopsy, but he's been there a few days, maybe more."

"What kind of weapon?"

"Same as the other one—sharp blade. He was sliced clean and easy."

"Was he killed there, or left there afterward?"

"Can't be sure. Either way there was a hell of a lot of blood."

"Yeah," I said, remembering what Jenny Wheeler had looked like in that cheap hotel room. "How'd you find out about this one?"

"Oh, I keep my ears open."

"I appreciate the call, Hocus."

"Sure. How's your girl?"

"She's not—she's fine. I've got Ray Carbone sitting on her."

"She should be safe then," he said. "Hope I didn't spoil your meal."

He had, but I said he hadn't and hung up.

$\triangledown$

3 4

WHEN I LEFT BOGIE'S it was nearly midnight. I was filled to the gills with coffee, wondering if it wouldn't have been better to be drunk. Binky was a snitch, and most of the time he was a lowlife, but in spite of that I had liked him. He had the charm of the rake, which often stood him in good stead with women, and sometimes charmed men, as well—and I don't mean in a sexual way. He was just a likable guy, and now he was dead.

Why?

And why was Andy McWilliams dead, if he wasn't a victim of the Backshooter?

I knew why Jenny Wheeler was dead. That one wasn't so hard. She was dead because she could have cleared Salvatore Scalesi of a murder charge—or because she could have convicted him.

I was sitting on two cases here, when under normal

circumstances I was just competent enough to work on one
at a time. My paying job was finding out who killed Jenny
Wheeler. And how had I gotten roped into that? I mean,
murder is a cop's job. Still, if I'd been a little quicker, maybe
Jenny wouldn't be dead.

To be painfully honest, the Wheeler case was at a dead
end. All I could do in the morning was to start canvassing
Jenny's friends to see if anyone knew anything. Maybe she
had bragged to someone that she had blown a real Mafia
Don.

As for the other case, there seemed to be no one who could
tell me anything but Andy McWilliams himself—or Andy's
ghost. I could find Andy's ghost in one of two places, I
thought: his office, or the office in his apartment. If I found
information that could get me killed, I'd keep it close to me.

I hailed a cab and gave the driver Caroline's home address,
fingering the key in my pocket. I had some communing to
do with a ghost.

35

I FELT FUNNY LETTING myself into the McWilliams apartment. I mean, I was there looking for a ghost, and if the ghost of Andy McWilliams was there, then he had heard his wife proposition me that night. Granted, I had turned her down, but a ghost could still take that personally, couldn't he?

I walked down the hall to the dining room and left the keys on the table. The last time Caroline had gone out she'd left a lamp on in the living room and, from the looks of it, in the bedroom as well. At least, that was what I thought at the time.

I considered going into the kitchen for a Paulie Girl, but decided against it. Instead I headed straight for the office.

As I moved into the doorway I saw the mess the office was in. Drawers had been pulled out and emptied onto the floor and books had been swept from the bookshelves. Obviously the room had been searched, and with an eye more toward thoroughness than neatness.

It was at times like this I wished I carried a gun.

I moved slowly into the office, but quickly realized that there was no place in the room that anyone could hide. Whoever had searched the office was gone.

Or so I thought, until something came crashing down on the back of my head to prove me wrong. Believe me, there are easier ways to be proven wrong.

3 6

I DRAGGED MYSELF UP off the floor and into Andy
McWilliams's swivel chair. I hoped his ghost wouldn't mind.
Who was I kidding? He was probably laughing at me uproar-
iously. Sure, pal, there was no room for anyone to hide in
the office, so the dude came out of the bedroom and laid you
out.

Good move.

I sat back, head loose on my neck, and waited to see if the
back of my head was going to fall off. When it didn't I put
my hand back there and was gratified to feel that there was
no blood. A lump, but I could live with that.

I got up and went to the kitchen for some ice. I filled a
towel with it, held it to the back of my head, and went back
to the office. Once again I sat in Andy's chair and surveyed
the carnage.

Andy had been killed months ago. Why search his office

now? I couldn't figure it, unless Caroline or I had simply pressed the right button on somebody.

I looked around the office, which, of course, I had intended to search myself, and wondered where I could look that hadn't already been searched.

I became aware of an odd whirring sound and realized that the desk top had been swept clean, including the phone. I picked it up and put the receiver in place and the noise stopped. I kept my hand on it, still looking the office over. Even the few framed pictures that had been on the wall had been thrown to the floor. There was broken glass all around, as well as pages that had been torn from books, obviously in frustration.

Where could I look that they hadn't already looked? The answer, of course, was right under my hand. The phone. Andy's phone, with all those one-touch buttons on it. I pulled the phone over to me and scanned his abbreviations. I ignored the obvious ones and concentrated on the one that had intrigued me on my first visit: "Tower."

Actually that was no longer such an obscure reference. It *could* have meant the Trump Tower. If that was it, why would he have put it on his phone? He hadn't worked on the Van Voorhies case himself. I would have expected the numbers he put into his one-touch system to be the ones he used frequently. Of course, he could have had other clients in the Tower, but I don't set much store in coincidence.

I was starting to get a bad feeling. I went on to some of the other entries. I looked again at the one that said "Don." Because of the way I'd spent my last few days, I read that now not as a proper name but as a title, as in Don Salvatore Scalesi.

The entry for "P.D." was probably somebody in the police department with his finger on the pulse of things, maybe a Deputy Inspector. My only legitimate contact was Hocus, a Detective First Class. That was the difference between Andy and me. I had no Trump Tower number in my book, nor did I have any Mafia Dons or Deputy Inspectors.

I saw nothing else of interest, I stood up, preparing to leave, and was hit by a wave of dizziness. I sat back down and decided there and then to spend the night where I was. In the morning I could try Andy's one-touch buttons and see who answered.

I woke once during the night, drenched in a cold sweat and without the faintest idea why. I got up and staggered to the bathroom and threw some cold water on my face. When that didn't clear my head I stripped and showered. As I dried myself I could smell Caroline on the towel, and suddenly I had a painful erection. I dressed again carefully and went into the kitchen for a glass of cold orange juice.

Suddenly, standing in the kitchen in my bare feet, I remembered the dream. I had dreamt that Andy McWilliams appeared to me in his bedroom and spoke to me. I couldn't remember what he had said—whether he had told me who killed him, or was warning me to get out of his bed and out of his apartment.

I looked longingly at the bottles of beer Caroline had bought for me, then drank a second glass of orange juice and went back to sleep, this time on a sofa in the living room.

37

I WOKE THE NEXT morning with my joints stiff and my head aching. I checked my watch and saw that it was ten o'clock. I was surprised I had slept so late. I went to the bathroom and took another shower. Then I found some Tylenol in the medicine cabinet and took three.

Thus fortified, I went back to the office and sat behind the desk, pulling the phone right up close to me.

I tried to decide which number to try first. The button marked "Don" beckoned to me. If it *was* Scalesi's number, however, nobody was going to just pick up the phone and announce, "Don Salvatore Scalesi's residence, local chapter of Murder Inc., wives a specialty."

I swiveled the chair around and looked out the window at the building across the way. There seemed to be a room full of mannequins just opposite the window, most of them undressed and bald, which was, I guess, the natural state of a mannequin.

If Andy McWilliams had a private number of Don Salvatore Scalesi's, wouldn't it stand to reason that he was a regular on Scalesi's payroll? And if that were the case, wouldn't it make Andy McWilliams well and truly *bent*? And what did that make Caroline? Surely Andy couldn't have been working for the Mafia without her knowing about it.

I turned the chair back around, lifted the receiver, and pressed the button marked "Tower." It rang three times and then a woman's voice said, "Van Voorhies, Ltd."

"Sorry," I said, and hung up.

I stared at the button marked "Don" and suddenly knew how to play it. I lifted the receiver and pressed the button. It ran seven times, but I was patient—and ultimately rewarded.

"Yes," said a man's voice.

"Tell Scalesi I can help him."

"What?"

"He wants to know who did Two-John Wheeler."

There was a sharp intake of breath as the party on the other end wondered how to play it.

"Who is this?" he finally asked.

"A friend."

"How did you get this number?" he demanded.

"I told you," I said. "I'm a friend. Tell the Don to be ready to deal when I call back."

"Just have somebody by the phone," I said, and hung up.

I looked across the way at the plastic people and wished at that moment I had the same problems they had—plastic ones.

I stood up, preparing to leave. I wanted to get some breakfast before the Tylenol made my empty stomach sick. Just for fun, before I left I picked up the phone and pressed the button marked "P.D."

"Task Force," a man's voice said after three rings.

"Task Force?" I said. "What Task Force?"

"The Backshooter Task Force," the man's voice said.

It was familiar, but I couldn't place it at the moment. "Who is this?"

"Detective Vandala!" the man said, annoyed now. "Who the hell is this?"

"Sorry," I said, and hung up before *he* recognized *my* voice.

Why the hell did Andy McWilliams have the number of the Backshooter Task Force on his system? Was Andy a victim of the Backshooter after all?

38

BEFORE LEAVING THE MCWILLIAMS apartment I threw the towels I had used into a hamper and looked around to see what I should clean up. As I passed the office I once again went in and picked up the phone. I called Walker Blue's office to make an appointment with his secretary to see him later that afternoon. I wouldn't take no for an answer, so she finally told me to come in at three o'clock. I hung up, looked at the condition of the office again, and laughed at my attempt to clean up after myself. What the hell was the difference?

I left and stopped at the first diner I came to. I ordered a breakfast special of scrambled eggs, bacon, and potatoes, with toast, coffee, and orange juice for $2.79. More than some places, less than others.

Feeling better for having eaten, I took the IRT subway down to Fourteenth Street, went home, and changed into fresh clothes. I put on a pot of coffee and called Hocus.

"Who do you know uptown?"

"Where?"

"The McWilliams apartment."

"I know somebody up there. Why?"

"The place has been broken into and searched."

"How do you know?"

"I was up there last night."

"How'd you get in?"

"I had a key."

"Oh, really."

"I took it from Caroline's hospital room while she was asleep."

"Oh, *really*?"

"Shut up, Hocus," I said. "She would have given it to me if she'd been awake—and *don't* say 'oh really' again."

"I'll give it to the boys up there. Any chance for prints?"

"It was a mess," I said, "but I think it was a pro job. You probably wouldn't find any prints."

"Except yours."

"Mine are on file," I said. "If they do find anything, let me know, huh?"

"They'll have to go to the hospital and talk to Mrs. McWilliams."

"I'll call Ray Carbone. He can tell her all about it."

"You, uh, didn't happen to walk in on the party, did you?"

"As a matter of fact," I said, putting my hand to the back of my head, "I did, but all I got for it was a headache."

"Didn't get a look at him?"

"Not even a peek."

"Now comes the big question."

"I don't know what they were looking for."

"And what were *you* looking for?"

"Um . . . " I said.

"That's what I thought."

"No, actually, I don't know what I was looking for, if you want the absolute truth."

"If I wanted the absolute truth—" he started to say, then stopped and said, "Never mind. Keep in touch, huh? I'd like to be able to get to you if the bodies of any more of your friends show up." He must have thought about Packy then because his voice changed and he said, "Jesus, Jack, I'm sorry."

"Forget it," I said. "I know what you mean. I'll be in touch."

I hung up and got a cup of coffee. I called Heck's office and Missy put me through to him. I told him about Binky.

"Jesus, Jack, what's going on?"

"Looks like someone wants your client to swing, Heck."

"They'll have to get in line."

"Are you up for a few questions?"

"Sure," he said, "I'll do my best to answer them in my finest lawyerly fashion."

"Geez," I said, "I'd prefer straight answers."

"Up yours."

"Did Andy McWilliams do any work for you on the Scalesi case?"

"No."

"Do you know if Andy did any work for Scalesi directly."

"That I don't know."

"Do you know a man named Jules Van Voorhies?"

"I know *of* him," Heck said. "Why are you asking me that?"

"I don't know," I said. "I must be getting desperate."

"Did you talk to Scalesi?"

"I did."

"What did you think?"

"I think he killed his wife." That met with silence. Why not? It even surprised me.

"Or had her killed." More silence. "Did you know he calls you a spic lawyer?"

"It doesn't surprise me."

"How can you defend him?"

"Money."

"And fame, if you get him off."

"I was never against fame."

I remembered once upon a time when fame was an idea I had, too. When I was in the ring.

"Me neither."

"Any more questions?"

"Probably," I said. "I'll call when I think of them."

"I've got one."

"Shoot."

"What did you say when he called me a spic lawyer?"

"I told him to get his minorities straight," I said. "I told him you were a wetback."

"It's nice to know my friends are there to defend me. When this is all over, how about dinner?"

"On you?"

"Of course."

"I'll have my girl call your girl." I said, and we hung up.

I poured myself another cup of coffee and then sat back down, wondering what the hell I had here. I was involved in what I thought were two cases, the Scalesi case and the McWilliams case. Jules Van Voorhies had come into play in the McWilliams case, but now I knew Andy McWilliams had a connection with both Van Voorhies and Scalesi.

It was noon. I decided to take a two hour nap before going to see Walker Blue, who, I hoped, would be able to shed light on some part of this puzzle.

$\triangledown$

39

WALKER BLUE'S SECRETARY WASN'T thrilled to see me, but she told him I was there and allowed me to enter.

"I heard about Caroline McWilliams," Blue said as I entered. "How is she?"

"Coming along," I said. "She could have been worse."

"Who did it?"

"We don't know," I said, and then added, "for sure."

"You have a theory?"

"I think it might have something to do with Andy McWilliams's death."

"After all this time?"

"There's a lot happening after all this time," I said, and told him about Andy's office being searched.

"Are you sure it wasn't just a burglary?"

"There was too much stuff left behind," I said, "and Andy's office was the only room that was gone through."

"I suppose you're here because you think I can help you," he said. His tone clearly indicated that he didn't think he could.

"I'm hoping you can," I said. "You and Andy did a lot of work together."

"Not quite," he said. "We referred a lot of work back and forth. Handled each other's overflow."

"Overflow," I repeated. "There's a word I'm not familiar with in this business."

"You will be."

"Tell me about Jules Van Voorhies, Walker."

He hesitated a moment, then said, "What about him?"

"I think there's a good chance he had Caroline worked over."

"For what purpose?"

"To scare her."

He considered that for a moment, then shook his head and said, "I don't see it."

"He tried to buy her off, and then he tried to buy me off. Neither of us went for it."

"Utilizing that logic," he said, "you're next in line for a beating."

"That's a possibility."

Blue paused for a moment. I suppose to consider what he was going to say next.

"Is it then your opinion that Van Voorhies had Andy killed, and that he was *not* a victim of the Backshooter?" he finally asked.

It was my turn to hesitate now as I formed the words carefully.

"I don't know that it's my *opinion*," I said, "but I've never been as strongly disposed toward that possibility as I am right now."

"How do you propose to . . . resolve this?"

"I guess that has a lot to do with you, Walker."

"Me?"

I nodded.

"You conducted the investigation into Van Voorhies's past," I said. "You must have found out what he's afraid of."

Blue didn't comment.

"Was it something that he would kill to keep secret?" I asked.

Again, Blue didn't comment.

"You know," he said after a moment, "it is true private investigators do not have a legal obligation of confidentiality, but nevertheless, I am predisposed towards loyalty to my clients."

"Loyalty to a client is fine," I said, "but we're talking about murder here. We're talking about having a *woman* beaten up, and who knows what his next move will be towards her—and *she* doesn't know anything."

"Have you told Van Voorhies that?" Blue asked. "And have you told him that *you* don't know anything?"

"I haven't told him anything," I said, "except that I can't be bought."

"Commendable."

"Let's stop fucking around Walker," I said, angrily. "What the fuck is Van Voorhies trying to hide? And if he killed Andy to cover it up, why hasn't he tried to kill you?"

"Good question, Jacoby," Blue said. "Try answering that one yourself."

"I have reason to believe Andy might have been on a retainer from Van Voorhies," I said. "What about you?"

"I have several clients who keep me on an annual retainer, but Jules Van Voorhies is not one of them."

"Did you report the findings of your investigation to Van Voorhies, or to Andy?"

"Both," Blue said.

Suddenly, I remembered something Blue had told me at some point.

"Walker, you said that you didn't like Van Voorhies, and that you didn't complete the job on him. Who did complete it?"

"I believe Andy did it himself," Blue said. "By the time I decided I no longer wanted to work on it, he seemed to have acquired the time to do it himself."

"Then correct me if I'm wrong, but your report must have been inconclusive."

He mulled that over for a while, then grudgingly admitted, "That's correct."

"Well, Jesus Christ," I said, standing up, "why didn't you tell me that in the first place?"

"I wasn't sure why you wanted to see my records. Andy McWilliams must have kept his own."

"No," I said, "no, for all intents and purposes there was no file." I explained to him what we had found in the Van Voorhies file.

"Walker," I said, afterward, "I suggest you let me have a look at that file anyway."

He chewed on that for a while and then said, "If it will help you find out who really killed Andy McWilliams . . . I'll have it brought out to the front desk."

"Fine," I said, "I'll just wait out there for it."

"Fine."

I walked to the door, then turned. I was probably more annoyed with Walker Blue than I had ever been before, which is saying something. I respected his abilities as a detective, but he *was* something of a snob most of the time.

"Listen," I said before leaving, "if I need any more help on this, I'll get right in touch with you. You've been real helpful."

$\triangledown$

40

I LEFT WALKER BLUE'S office with his Van Voorhies report beneath my arm. When I reached the street I suddenly remembered that I had not fed Ray Carbone's cat. Before going home to read the file I stopped by Ray's West Village apartment and let myself in with the key Ray had given me. Okay, it wasn't original, but Ray was never blessed with great flashes of originality. It was one of his problems in the ring.

I fed the beautiful grey and white Persian cat, shaking my head at how many different varieties of cat food Ray had in his cupboard. You really wouldn't expect a guy like Ray to have a cat, Persian or otherwise. A bulldog maybe, but not a cat.

Having fed the animal, who attacked the food voraciously. I left Ray's and went back to my own apartment. There I read Walker Blue's report. It was really useless, except for a line Blue had added to the end.

"It is my belief that Jules Van Voorhies might have, at some time in his early career, had some contact with the Mafia, but I cannot document that at this time, nor can I supply the name of a possible contact."

I guess it fell to Andy to pursue that further, prove it, and come up with a name. If he had, then what name had he come up with?

Given the amount of coincidence I'd had to swallow up to this point, maybe *I* could supply a name. How about Don Salvatore Scalesi? Would an uncovered personal relationship with Scalesi be enough to threaten Van Voorhies's political career? What if he still had a relationship with Scalesi? Couldn't the Don's political connections *help* Van Voorhies get into office?

What if Van Voorhies had been the one to sever the connection? Even if he had, the Mafia would not reveal it. They wouldn't want to ruin his chances to get into office, because once he *was* in office, he'd find out that no one ever completely ends their relationship with the Mafia. Once they've got you by the throat, they don't let go. And once Van Voorhies was in office, he'd probably do anything to stay there.

That meant that if he had been foolish enough to have Andy killed to cover up his connection with Scalesi—or with the Mafia in general—then Andy had been killed for no reason.

Maybe I should try telling Van Voorhies that. Maybe I should call him and tell him I had evidence and see what that made him do. Granted, that wasn't detective work, but I knew a guy in Boston who did that all the time. Rather than try to find some definite evidence, he simply pushed and prodded until the guilty party came after him.

Before I approached Van Voorhies with a threat of evidence, though, I wanted to try to get some real evidence in my hot little hand. That meant I had to go see Caroline again.

4 1

Ray CARBONE WAS STILL seated in that same plastic chair in front of Caroline's room, and for a man who had been on twenty-four hour call he looked remarkably awake.

"Did you feed the cat?" was the first thing he asked me.

"Of course I fed the cat," I said. "What do you take me for?"

"He gets testy if he misses a meal."

"Well, we wouldn't want him getting testy, would we?" I asked, relieved that I had remembered in time. "How is everything here?"

"Fine," he said. "I had a nurse buy a newspaper and I took it in to her. I think your girl is ready to go home."

I didn't correct him about Caroline being "my girl."

"I'll talk to her," I said, patting him on the shoulder and going on in.

"Jack!" she said as I entered. She was sitting up in bed reading the paper.

"What's the good word?"

"I've got five for you," she said, "Get-me-out-of-here!"

"What do the doctors say?"

"Another couple of days."

"Then I guess you'll be staying another couple of days."

"But I want to get out of here and help you, Jack," she said. "You need me."

"You can stay right where you are and help me a lot, Caroline."

"How?"

I told her about the apartment being broken into and the office being ransacked. I did not tell her about being conked on the head, or that I had spent the night there and seen Andy's ghost.

"But what were they looking for?"

"I think they were looking for more papers on Jules Van Voorhies."

"After all this time?"

"They may not have wanted to break into your home so soon after Andy's death," I said.

"But if they removed the papers from the file in the office, why break into the apartment?"

"They *didn't* get what they wanted then," I said.

"What do you mean? Did they find it in the apartment? There wasn't anything else in—"

"I think Andy found out something that was so hot he decided to hide part of the file. He's the one who removed the contents."

"Did he hide it in the apartment?" she asked. "Did they find it?"

"Maybe not," I said. "Andy'd be too smart to hide it in the office or the apartment. Caroline, where *would* Andy hide something like that?"

She thought a moment then looked hopeless and said, "I don't know."

"Think about it," I said. "Think *hard*."

She frowned, thinking, and eventually gave up with a shrug.

"If Andy had a secret hiding place, it's news to me."

"Were you close, Caroline?" I asked. "I mean, wouldn't you have known something like that?"

"Jack," she said. "I knew a lot of things about Andy, but we really weren't what you'd call a close couple. I mean . . . I knew he was seeing other women."

"He, uh, was?"

She smiled and said, "You know it too, don't you?"

"Uh . . . "

"Sure," she said, "you must have seen him once or twice with a woman."

"Well . . . "

"Never mind," she said, touching my hand.

"Caroline," I said, suddenly getting an idea, "did Andy have a *particular* woman?"

"If he did he kept that from me as well," she said. "All I know is that there were telltale signs that he had been with other women, but I don't know whether it was one or twenty-one. Why?"

"Well, if he *did* have one woman, he might have left the file with her."

She stared down at her hands and said, "I can't help you with that."

"Who could?" I asked. "Who were Andy's close friends?"

"We didn't have a lot of friends," she said. "At least, not in common. If you're asking if Andy had an asshole buddy he'd confide in, I don't think so. He wasn't that type."

I waited for more, but there wasn't anymore forthcoming.

I leaned over and kissed her gently on the forehead.

"Do what the doctors tell you."

"That's the second time you've done that."

"What?"

"Kissed me like we were brother and sister," she said accusingly. "Don't you know any other way to kiss?"

I stared at her for a moment, then leaned forward and kissed her on the mouth. She had a soft, yielding mouth and she tasted faintly medicinal, but the kiss went on for some time.

When it was over I said, "See ya, Sis," and got out of there.

I think I heard her yell, "Chicken!" as I was going out the door.

42

I WENT TO BOGIE'S for dinner. Vivian gave me a big welcome as I entered, and I told her I'd take a table rather than sit at the bar this time. She led me to my usual table—when I used a table—in the center of the wall opposite the bar. At table one there was a group of people, and I thought one of them looked familiar.

"What's going on over there?" I asked.

"A bunch of mystery people," she said. "Well, actually the table is being paid for by an editor, a friend of Billy and Karen's from the Mystery Writers."

"What's his name?"

"Seidman."

"Which is he?"

"The man with the glasses, sitting against the wall," she said.

"Wasn't he here with a party before?"

"Yes," she said, "and he's here again."

Suddenly I didn't like the man, but maybe it was because I didn't have what he had—a large group of people hanging on my every word. I had friends, but you wouldn't have found them sitting at a big round table with me. Chances are my friends wouldn't like each other. I'm lucky they like me.

I ordered dinner and was just starting to eat when Billy came out of his office in the back. Once upon a time it had doubled as my office and I still used it sometimes for privacy. There hadn't been very much need for privacy of late. Business wasn't booming, and what would Dicky Hilary make of that?

I suddenly realized that was the first time in a long while I had thought of Dicky and what happened in court—and it didn't bother me as much. I guess Packy's death and Caroline getting beat up made me realize there are worse things in life than being made to look like a fool.

Billy came over to the table.

"Hi, Jack."

"Hi, Billy," I said. "Have a seat."

"Let me get a coffee first." He went to where the coffee pots were and poured himself a glass. He always drank his coffee from a glass rather than a cup. He added milk and sugar and then carried it over and sat down.

"So, how are you?" he asked.

"Confused."

"I meant what's *new*."

"Very funny."

"Bad case?"

"Two of them."

"Hey, business is looking up. Maybe you'll be able to pay your tab."

I frowned and said, "I'm not sure, but I think I'm only getting paid for one of them."

"Well," he said with a fatalistic shrug, "there goes this month's rent. Anything I can help with?"

Billy was always after me to let him help me on one of my cases.

"I'd like some help," I said, "but I don't think there's anything you can do for me right now."

He snapped his fingers and said, "Yes there is." He started to get up as he said, "I can give you your messages."

He walked to the bar and asked for the bartender—whose name was Killian—for my messages, then walked back and handed me a piece of paper.

"Thanks."

"Maybe that'll be something that will help."

"I hope so," I said. I read it and saw that a woman named Linda Matella had called me. Whoever had written the message had underlined the word "urgent."

"So?"

"Potential client, I think," I said. "Who took the message?"

"Killian."

"Excuse me."

I got up and walked to the bar. Killian was a medium height, dark-haired man with a pleasant Irish accent that the ladies ate up.

"Killian, what do you know about this message?"

"The lady said it was very important, Jack."

"Did she say who she was?"

"I wrote her name—"

"I mean, beyond that. Did she say what it was about?"

"Let me think," he said. "It came in earlier this evening. She said that she had something for you, and that it was very important she get in touch with you."

"She has something for me?"

"Yes."

"Did she say what?"

"No."

"Did she say anything else?"

"I don't think—wait a minute. She said to tell you that it used to be Andy's."

The name hit me like a cold shower.

"Andy?" I repeated. "You're sure she said Andy?"

"Positive."

I looked at the message again. Linda Matella, 877-0714. "877, Killian," I said. "Where's that prefix from?"

He thought a moment, then said, "There's a bar uptown with that prefix. It's on Amsterdam, in the Eighties."

"Thanks. I need the phone."

He brought me the wireless and I impatiently punched out the number. It rang four times and I was starting to worry that she might not be in, but the phone was picked up in the middle of the fifth ring.

"Hello?"

"Linda Matella?"

"Yes."

"This is Miles Jacoby."

"Finally," she said, with impatience.

"I've been very busy and unable to get back to you," I said.

"I know you've been busy, Mr. Jacoby," she said. "I read about Caroline in the papers, and I know you're helping her."

"Do you know Caroline?"

"Uh . . . no," she said, "I've never met her, but Andy talked about her a lot."

"You knew Andy?" I said, stupidly. She'd just said she did.

"Mr. Jacoby," she said, "I knew Andy very well."

Her meaning was clear. Without even looking I had found Andy's girlfriend, and she had something for me.

If I hadn't been so stupid, I could have had it a week ago.

$\triangledown$

43

LINDA MATELLA LIVED UPTOWN, on West End between Eighty-second and Eighty-third. I caught a cab on the corner of Eighth Avenue and Twenty-sixth and sat impatiently through a twenty minute cab ride. Luckily it was getting dark and there was less traffic than there would have been during the day.

I overtipped the cabbie in my haste to get where I was going, entered the lobby, and pressed the buzzer marked 5C *L. Matella*.

"Yes?" her distorted voice said through the intercom.

"Miles Jacoby."

She buzzed me in and I had another impatient ride, this time in the slow-moving elevator. When it reached five I shoved the door open and made a right turn. Right there next to the elevator, was 5C and I pressed the bell. I could hear her footsteps on a hardwood floor, and then the door swung open.

Bingo, I thought. Unless I had a bad memory for flashy blondes, this was the blonde who had been on Andy's arm that time in Canada.

"You look familiar," I said.

"So do you," she said. "Come on in."

She was tall, about five-ten, and she was wearing heels, so she stood taller than me. She was the beauty contest type, her blonde hair long and luxurious, full of body—and speaking of body! Hers wouldn't quit, as they say. In fact, she might have been too buxom to be the ideal beauty contest contestant. I read someplace that the bust sizes of Miss Americas and Miss Universes were going down. Maybe their I.Q.s were coming up.

"Go on inside," she said, interrupting my thoughts as she closed the door. I walked into the apartment ahead of her.

"Can I get you a drink?" she asked.

"No, thanks. Your message said you had something for me. Something that used to be Andy's?"

"Yes, I do. Listen, can we go in the kitchen? I was just putting on some pasta."

"Sure," I said, and followed her to the kitchen. She definitely had that runway type of walk, which had probably been turning heads since she was a teen. She appeared to me to be about twenty-eight or so. She was wearing a tight black skirt and a pink blouse. If it wasn't for the fact that she was putting on a pot of pasta I would have thought she was going out.

Obviously she was expecting someone in.

The kitchen smelled of meat sauce and spices.

"Listen," I said, "I can see you're expecting company—"

"Just a friend," she said. "Would you like to join us for dinner?"

"No, thanks," I said, becoming impatient. "I just want to pick up what you have for me."

"It's there," she said from the stove, "on the kitchen table."

I walked over to the table and picked up a number 10 white envelope, the kind you get mail in every day. From the feel of it, it contained quite a few pages. The front was blank.

The answers are in here, I thought. But the answers to what?

"How long did you know Andy?" I asked. Suddenly, I was wary of opening the envelope.

She turned from the stove and looked at me.

"Are you good friends with Caroline—Mrs. McWilliams?"

"I suppose you could say we're friends," I said.

"But not old friends?"

"No."

"You're not going to judge me, or anything? I mean, I know carrying on with a married man isn't the coolest thing to do, but—well, you knew Andy. He was a very charming man."

"Yes, I know."

"You were at that convention, weren't you?" she asked. "In Canada?"

"Yes."

"That's where I saw you." she said. "Well, that was what—two years ago? I'd known Andy about a year then."

"You met after he was married?"

She frowned and said, "I thought you weren't going to judge me."

"I'm not . . . I'm sorry . . . " I said, but my sputtering was cut off by the bell.

"He's early," she said frowning. "Excuse me."

"I should go—" I said.

"Please," she said, "have a glass of wine or something."

"All right."

"Excuse me," she said again, and went to answer the door.

I debated opening the envelope while she was gone, but I finally decided to stuff it in my jacket pocket. I had just done so when I heard footsteps approaching the kitchen. More than two sets . . .

I turned and saw Linda come staggering into the room, obviously on the wrong end of a push. She was followed by two men, both of whom had shoulders that filled the doorway.

"Jacoby, right?" one of them asked.

"I assume neither of these gentlemen is your date?" I said to Linda.

"I don't know these two jokers," she said. "They pushed their way in here—"

"Shut up, sweetheart," the first man said. He looked like the star of that TV series, "Wiseguy," only not as good-looking.

"What do you guys want?"

"There's a little matter of a file, pal," Wiseguy's partner said. He looked like the guy who used to play "Jethro," on "The Beverly Hillbillies," only not as good-looking. They were both wearing long, black coats. They looked like undertakers. I wondered if that was an omen.

"What file?"

"Don't play games, Jacoby," Wiseguy said. "The file our boss is getting tired of looking for. The one we went to Bogie's to ask you for. You was leaving, and we followed you here. Now we're asking . . . give us the file."

"Fellas," I said, "I don't know what—"

Wiseguy clapped his hand down on my shoulder hard, cutting me off.

"Let's go someplace where we can be more comfortable, and talk about it, huh?"

I gave the kitchen a quick once over, looking for something to use as a weapon. My eyes came to rest on an aerosol can on top of the refrigerator, which was next to the stove. It was probably air freshener, but that didn't matter. I was more concerned with the fact that it was an aerosol can. I had to do this right.

"Let's go," Wiseguy said.

"Where?" I asked.

"Into the living room, for now," he said. "We might as well get comfortable while we . . . negotiate."

"Let's go," Jethro echoed.

"Linda?" I said, indicating that she should go first.

Both Wiseguy and Jethro betrayed their upbringing by standing aside so she could go first. Wiseguy followed, eyeing her ass.

"You too, pal," Jethro said.

"I'm coming," I said, wondering how I was going to get ahold of that aerosol can.

I went through the kitchen door ahead of him, and he followed. There wasn't much space for me to get by him, but I turned quickly and pushed past him back into the kitchen.

"Hey!" he shouted.

I ignored him, hoping he wouldn't shoot me in the back. I grabbed the aerosol can and quickly dropped it into the pot of water Linda had started to boil for the pasta, then turned to face him as he charged into the kitchen after me with a gun in his hand.

"What the fuck?" he said.

"I want to turn off the stove," I said. "The water might boil over."

"Fuck the water, friend," he shouted, spraying me with spittle. He pushed the barrel of the gun under my chin and said, "I should blow your fucking head off."

"Don't kill him," Wiseguy shouted from the living room, "just bring him the fuck in here!"

"Move, damn it!" Jethro said. He grabbed my jacket and propelled me towards the door. "Shut off the water," he muttered, walking behind me. "What a dipshit!"

In the living room Linda was sitting on the edge of a sofa. I was sort of surprised at how calm she was—surprised and pleased. When it came time to move, maybe she wouldn't fall apart on me.

$\bigtriangledown$

44

"Now," WISEGUY SAID, "LET'S do this the easy way, okay?"

"Okay," I said. "What's the easy way?"

"The easy way,"he said, "is for the lady here to give us what we want."

"Not much chance of that, dickbreath," Linda said.

I closed my eyes. Just what I needed, a woman who used to watch "Hillstreet Blues" and thought Mick Belker was cute.

"Ooh," Wiseguy said, "I just love a tough talkin' broad. Don't you love a tough talkin' broad?" he asked his friend.

"No," Jethro said, "I don't."

I noticed they were being careful not to call each other by name. Still, that didn't mean they wouldn't kill us after they got what they wanted, it only meant that they were being pros.

"I take it that means you want to do this the hard way," Wiseguy said to her.

I answered before she could. There was no telling *what* she was going to call him this time.

"That depends," I said. "What's the hard way?"

"The hard way," Wiseguy said, "is when my friend here takes the lady into her bedroom and fucks the shit out of her until one of you gives us what we want."

I looked at Jethro, whose eyes were shining as he undressed Linda with his eyes. He cupped his balls and said to her, "That's *really* the hard way."

"Your dick wouldn't interest me in a million years, asswipe."

Asswipe?

"Believe me, honey," Jethro said, shifting his gun to his left hand and taking her by the arm and yanking her to her feet with his right, "you're gonna love this."

"Now wait a minute—" I said as Jethro starting dragging her away.

"Yeah, wait a minute," Wiseguy said.

"What for?" Jethro demanded.

"Well, I don't want to spoil your fun," Wiseguy said to his friend, "but there might be a faster way to do this."

"Like how?" Jethro asked.

"Yeah, like how?" I echoed.

I was wondering if I had remembered wrong about aerosol cans. Wasn't there a warning on the back of the can to keep them away from extreme heat? And I had one in a pot of boiling water!

"Well," Wiseguy said, "if the lady has already *given* Jacoby what we want, then it will be on him. And if it's on him, then it's as good as ours."

He was very pleased with his logic.

I, on the other hand, was not.

"I don't have anything, partner," I said, "but feel free to search me."

The damned envelope was burning a hole in my pocket!

He frowned, puzzled for a moment, but then he brightened.

"Play it to the hilt, friend," he said, moving towards me. "Come on, get up. I want to go through your pockets."

"I know how your friend gets his jollies," I said, standing, "is this how you get yours?"

"Keep laughing, pal," he said, grinning, "because pretty soon you're gonna get *yours*."

He was still grinning, reaching for my jacket pockets, when there was an explosion from the kitchen.

Linda moved faster than I did, lifting her knee and planting it in Jethro's crotch. I don't know if she scored a bull's-eye, but it was hard enough to double him over, anyway. She pushed him then and he fell backward, landing on her glass coffee table and going through it.

I grabbed Wiseguy's lapels and pulled him towards me, butting him with my head. He cried out as I pushed him aside.

"Run!" I shouted to Linda.

45

I KNOW WHAT YOU'RE thinking.

I've watched this scene a lot on TV shows, too. I always ask myself why the hero runs instead of bending over to pick up the bad guy's gun. Now I understand. Running is an instinct, and in adverse situations, people act on instinct.

Also, Jethro hadn't let go of his gun when he fell. We would have had to wrestle with him to try to get it away from him. It was better for all concerned—especially Linda and me—to put as much distance between us and them as we could.

I grabbed her hand and we ran for the hall. I started to press the button for the elevator but she snapped, "Forget it!" and pulled me to the stairs.

What the hell, it was only five flights, and I *did* use to be an athlete.

She was ahead of me on the stairs. I noticed that somewhere along the line she had kicked off her shoes. I was impressed with her coolness under fire. No wonder Andy liked her.

When we reached the main lobby I thought I heard someone shouting from the stairwell, and then I heard a shot.

"Shit," I said.

"Come on," she said, pulling me toward the front door.

When we got outside we stopped, trying to figure out which way to run.

"It's your neighborhood," I said.

"This way," she said, pulling me to the left.

We ran to Eighty-first street. I looked back once and saw Wiseguy and Jethro come running out of her building. We turned the corner then, but they might have seen us.

As she reached the corner of Eighty-first and Broadway I noticed there was a bookstore there, and it was open.

"Wait," I said to her, and ran into the bookstore, no doubt leaving her puzzled.

I approached the girl seated behind the desk where people were supposed to check their bags and handed her the envelope.

"I'd like to check this."

"Oh, that's all right," she said. "You only have to check bags and—"

"I *want* to check this!" I insisted.

She jumped at my harsh tone and quickly took the envelope and handed me half a playing card. She must have thought I was another New York sickie.

"Thank you," I said. I stuffed the card into my pocket and ran outside. I didn't look at it. If it was the ace of spades, I didn't want to know.

"What the hell—" Linda started, but I took her hand and said, "Later. Let's run."

We started running down Broadway and I was looking for a cop. Behind us I heard some yelling and I figured Wiseguy and Jethro were right on our tail.

I suddenly realized that *Linda* was pulling *me*. I was holding her back.

I released her hand and said, "Keep going."

She turned and said, "Come *on*," reaching for me, but I pulled by hands back from her.

"Keep going," I said. "Look for a cop."

She gave me an impatient look, then turned back around and ran. She steadily increased the distance between us even though I was running as hard as I could—and she was wearing a skirt. Granted, she had hiked it up so she could take longer strides, but still . . .

I sneaked a look behind me and saw that even as Linda was increasing the distance between her and me, Wiseguy was *de*creasing the distance between *him* and me.

Shoot, I thought, I was a boxer. This bozo was probably a track star.

I looked ahead and could no longer see Linda. Good, maybe she'd turned a corner somewhere and was well on her way to getting away.

Now if only I could get lucky.

Lucky, hell. Just when I didn't need a cab I ran right into one. I was about to cross the street—I didn't know where we were. Seventy-seventh, maybe Seventy-sixth—when a cab pulled right in front of me and stopped for the light. I couldn't stop and ran right into the damned thing. I banged my knee, cried out, and then bounced off, losing my balance and falling to the pavement.

I tried to get up, but my knee wouldn't cooperate, and then I was hit from behind. Wiseguy and I rolled around for a while and then suddenly I heard a woman shout, "Freeze, dirtbag!"

We stopped and I looked up. Somehow Linda had tripped Jethro as he went by, and he had skidded on the ground, dropping his gun, which she now held in a perfect military stance.

"I wouldn't move if I were you, pal," I said to Wiseguy.

"Fuck," he said, under his breath.

I was pleased to see that he was huffing and puffing just as much as I was. I reached into his jacket and relieved him of his gun, then limped over to where Linda was standing. Jethro was lying on his back and his face was a bloody mess as a result of his skid on the concrete.

"Are you all right?" she asked.

"I'm . . . fine," I said, leaning against the wall behind her.

"Somebody call the police, please!" she shouted.

"Tell me . . . something," I said between panting.

"What?"

"Just what do you do for a living?"

"Oh, didn't I tell you?" she said. "I'm a cop!"

"A . . . cop?"

"Yes," she said, and proceeded to announce this fact to all of the bystanders, once again asking them to call the police.

"Where did you learn . . . *dirtbag*?" I asked. "Hill Street Blues?"

"No," she said, without looking at me, "Police Academy Two. Or was it Three?"

46

NOTHING TURNED OUT THE way I thought it would.

A week later Caroline and I were having dinner at Bogie's. There was still some color on her face from the bruises and she still had a bandage on her cheek and tape on her ribs, but she swore she was feeling a lot better.

That fella Seidman was sitting at what I found out was considered Table One with a whole group of mystery people—again. I thought that if I told *them* the way things had turned out, they'd think it was too unbelievable, even for fiction.

For one thing, when I went back to the bookstore to get the envelope, they had closed and I had to wait until the next morning to pick it up. Once I had it, though, I realized that it was Andy's report on Van Voorhies and his definite connection with Don Salvatore Scalesi. Andy had given the file to Linda Matella without telling her what it was. It had been Linda's idea to turn it over to me.

It was true that Linda was a cop, but she worked at Police Headquarters, collating facts and figures. That was how she'd met Andy. He had gone to Headquarters for some figures and Linda was the one he ended up talking to.

Caroline had made a lot of noise at Police Headquarters when Andy was first killed, and periodically she went back there and tried again. Before long, Linda became aware that Caroline was investigating Andy's death.

Linda had also felt that there was something fishy about Andy's death. Still, she had not thought anything of the envelope he'd left with her until recently. The contents meant nothing to her but she wanted to get it to Caroline without actually *talking* to Caroline, so she asked a detective friend of hers to find out about Caroline's investigation. The detective friend turned out to be friends with Detective Vadala from the Backshooter Task Force, who asked around and found out that I was helping Caroline.

"He wasn't very complimentary about you, Jack," she confided to me later, "but once I got your name I called Bogie's and left a message."

Vadala had apparently told her that I hung out at Bogie's.

When Linda heard about Caroline being beaten up she'd decided she had to call me. I had run up there so fast I hadn't even noticed I was being tailed by Van Voorhies men. He had gotten tired of looking for the file and had dispatched them to find me and see if I had it, once and for all. They had gone to Bogie's, and two other men had been sent to my house. When they arrived I was just leaving, and they had tailed me and broken in on Linda and me.

When Hocus confronted him, Van Voorhies fell apart like a cheap watch. He explained that Andy was blackmailing him. The file in the envelope had directly linked Van Voorhies to Scalesi, and that was what the man was trying to hide. He said that Andy wanted big corporate cases sent his way, and the big retainers that would go with it. He'd had my friend "Wiseguy"—whose name turned out to be Lenny Anderson—pull the trigger on Andy to avoid the blackmail.

I didn't tell this to Caroline. I told her that Van Voorhies was *afraid* that Andy was going to blackmail him. I didn't want to believe Van Voorhies myself, but why was there a button marked "Tower" on Andy's phone. That certainly indicated that he would be calling Van Voorhies regularly, didn't it? If I dug around some more, would I begin to nail the answer down?

I mean, that was like looking further to find out why Andy had a direct line to Scalesi? Perhaps Andy was just working regularly for the Don. Maybe Andy's practice was tapering off, and he had decided that politicians and Mafioso weren't so bad? Their money was green, too wasn't it? And Andy didn't seem now to have had as many scruples as we'd thought. If I looked further, would I find out?

Maybe I would. Maybe I'd find the answer to all of that, but did I want to prove to Caroline that her husband had turned into a blackmailer and a Mafia associate?

The answer to that was, shit no!

Her husband's murder had been solved, and she had been right all along. He had not been a victim of the Backshooter.

Let's just leave it at that.

"What about Scalesi?" she asked.

"He'll probably be convicted of killing his wife."

"Did he do it?"

"I don't know," I said. "His attorney doesn't know, either. I think he did."

"If he did it, why would he give Heck Two-John Wheeler's name as an alibi?"

"So maybe he didn't do it," I said, with a shrug. "So he serves time for something he didn't do. There's plenty that he *did* do. That's called balancing the scales of justice."

"I guess so," she said. "So who killed Two-John?"

"The cops have made an arrest on that. It was a bad john she had taken up there to turn some quick getaway money. Apparently, in her haste to build herself a big enough stake to get out of town, she wasn't very careful about who she was, uh, doing."

"How'd the cops get him?"

"He tried it on another hooker, and she stabbed him."

"Dead?"

"No, he'll likely serve time."

"Who was in her room when we got there?"

"I don't know, probably a junkie."

She started to look confused. I knew exactly how she felt. I had felt the same way when Hocus started explaining it all to me.

"So her murder was just a coincidence?"

"Looks that way."

"What if it *wasn't* the john who did it? What if one of Scalesi's men did it?"

"It doesn't matter, Caroline," I said. "Either way she's dead, and Scalesi's doing time."

"So Andy's death and Two-John's death were not related?"

"No."

"And Scalesi had nothing to do with Andy's death?"

"Nothing," I said. "Andy's case and Scalesi's were totally separate cases."

Did I believe that? Remember, I knew that Andy had a direct phone line to Scalesi *and* Van Voorhies. The fact that everything had been wrapped up didn't mean that it had all been wrapped up *right*.

Still, there was something to be said for things being wrapped up. Look at Binky's death. That had been closed out as Binky being killed by some poor homeless bozo in a fight over the box Binky'd been found in. Case closed, on all counts. Right or wrong.

What could I do about it? There was no fucking way anything could be confirmed for sure, so why beat my head against a stone wall?

Andy was dead. The rest of it wasn't important and I didn't want Caroline wondering about it for the rest of her life.

I couldn't keep Linda Matella from her, though, so I told her that Andy had left the file with Linda to safeguard, and she hadn't figured out what to do with it until now. Caroline didn't ask me any questions about Linda—like "What is she like?" or "What does she look like?"—for which I was grateful. Linda had asked me to call her sometime. I didn't know yet if I would. I mean, I liked *both* women . . .

There was just one other small question that had to be answered, about Andy having the Backshooter Task Force phone number on his phone. As it turned out, it wasn't the Task Force number so much as Detective Vadala's number. Vadala was Andy's P.D. contact, and didn't *that* surprise me, knowing how Vadala felt about P.I.s. Maybe it was just *me* Vadala disliked.

"Here," Caroline said.

I looked down and saw that she had slid a white number 10 envelope across the table from me.

"I've had enough trouble with envelopes," I said. "What's in this one?"

"Your fee."

"Oh."

I figured it out, deducting the days you, ah, weren't working."

The days I was drunk, or rescuing myself from becoming a *real* drunk.

"Caroline—" I said, touching the envelope but not picking it up.

"You're not going to argue with me about this, are you?" she asked. "You put a lot of time into this. You've got to be compensated."

"I was paid by Heck Delgado for the work I did on behalf of his client," I said.

"Well, take this anyway," she said. "Remember, I know how hard it is for a P.I. to make ends meet."

I tapped the envelope a few times and then said, "Oh, all right," and slid the envelope into my pocket, "but I'm buying dinner."

"Agreed."

Billy Palmer came into the dining room, looking like he was about to burst.

"What is it?" I asked.

"Did you hear?" he said, excitedly. "They caught the bastard!"

"Caught who?" Caroline asked.

"The Backshooter," Billy said. "They caught him."

"How?" I asked.

"He tried it again tonight, only his victim got *him* first. Get this, the guy was an off-duty cop!"

I sat stunned. The sonofabitch who killed Packy had finally picked on the wrong person.

"Is he dead?" I asked.

"Not yet," Billy said. "They've got him over at Bellevue, and they're working on him. Wasted effort, I say. They should let him die."

"I agree," I said. The faster the bastard died the quicker he'd burn in hell for what he did to Packy and the others.

"What a coincidence, huh?" Billy said. "Him picking on an off-duty cop?"

"Yep," I said, "some coincidence."

"This is big news," Billy said. "Excuse me." He started to walk away towards Table One and then stopped short. "Hey, Jack? Have you decided what you're going to do with Packy's?"

"Keep it open," I said. I'd thought long and hard about it. "It's home to a lot of people. I think Packy would want it to stay open."

"Well, welcome to the saloon business," he said. "Good luck."

Caroline and I sat in silence for a while, thinking things over.

Suddenly she said, "Come to dinner tomorrow night?"

I looked at her, an inch away from saying no, and then I said yes.

What the hell. She was a P.I. I was a P.I. That was a match made in heaven.

Right?

If you have enjoyed this book and would like to receive
details of other Walker mystery titles, please write to:

Mystery Editor
Walker and Company
720 Fifth Avenue
New York, NY 10019